DLR 7293

D1220248

"Oh, m-my-l-lord," Jean babbled. "The ghost!"

He hugged her, and the sensations that evoked were singularly pleasant, so he hugged her closer. "Calmly now," he said, "What ghost?"

"In the long gallery," Jean whispered. "The ghost of the gray lady."

Jean was not wearing any stays. Her body was soft and yielding under his comforting hands, which were stroking her back and were now itching to move round to her front. "And what did she look like?" he murmured against her hair, beginning to enjoy himself immensely and wondering whether a comforting kiss would be in order.

But Jean recovered enough to be aware that she was in, or rather on, the viscount's bed and that he was holding her very closely. She extricated herself and stood a little way from the bed in a shaft of moonlight that showed the viscount clearly the rise and fall of her excellent bosom. "I should not have burst in on you in this hurly-burly way," Jean said shakily. "But I am monstrous frightened."

Also by Marion Chesney
Published by Fawcett Books:

A GOVERNESS OF DISTINCTION

Marion Chesney

FAWCETT CREST • NEW YORK

Sale of this book without a front cover may be unauthorized. If this book is coverless, it may have been reported to the publisher as "unsold or destroyed" and neither the author nor the publisher may have received payment for it.

A Fawcett Crest Book
Published by Ballantine Books
Copyright © 1992 by Marion Chesney

All rights reserved under International and Pan-American Copyright Conventions. Published in the United States by Ballantine Books, a division of Random House, Inc., New York, and simultaneously in Canada by Random House of Canada Limited, Toronto.

Library of Congress Catalog Card Number: 92-90602

ISBN 0-449-21994-1

Manufactured in the United States of America

First Edition: December 1992

Chapter One

EVEN IN THE HEDONISTIC SOCIETY of Regency London, Percy, Viscount Hunterdon, stood out as being more carefree, indolent, and pleasure-loving than anyone else among the top thousand.

Although apparently destined to eke out his days on a small inheritance, he found he was lucky at gambling—very lucky—and was therefore able to live an extravagant life. He was extremely handsome with golden curly hair, bright blue eyes, and a tall athletic figure, for he boxed and fenced and raced his curricle, finding that a certain amount of exercise was excellent for dissipating the results of the previous night's roistering.

As he strolled along the Strand one sunny afternoon in the direction of Temple Bar, nothing disturbed the calm pool of his brain except for one little ripple which wondered what on earth old Mr. Courtney's lawyers wanted to see him about. Mr. Mirabel Courtney, he knew, was some very distant relative. He had never even met the old man. But now the lawyers had written a tetchy letter to the viscount to say that after repeated calls at his house and at his club without success, they suggested that if he wished to learn something to his advantage then he had better call on them.

1

He finally reached the musty offices of Triggs, Bellman, and Broome and airly announced his arrival to an elderly clerk who informed the viscount that Mr. Broome would see him.

Mr. Broome was like an elderly tortoise, his thin neck poking out of a painfully starched cravat and high-collared shirt.

"Old Courtney left me something, has he?" Lord Hunterdon demanded gaily.

"Sit down, my lord," Mr. Broome said severely. "There is more to it than that."

"Isn't there always?" The viscount slumped down in a chair and looked vaguely out of the window. "Spare me the heretofores and wherefroms and all that legal jargon and get to the point."

Mr. Broome sniffed loudly to show his disapproval and picked up a sheaf of papers. "Mr. Mirabel Courtney has left you his quite considerable fortune, Trelawney Castle in Dorset, and his estates," he said.

Lord Hunterdon blinked in surprise. "Well, very kind of him, to be sure. Fetch a good price, I should think."

"You cannot sell it," Mr. Broome remarked with a gleam of satisfaction in his watery old eyes. "In order to inherit, you must live in the castle and make it your home. Also . . ."

"Also?" the viscount echoed faintly.

"Also you must take charge of Mr. Courtney's daughters, Amanda and Clarissa, and find them husbands."

"How can anyone be expected to find husbands for a couple of old maids?"

"The Misses Courtney are fifteen-year-old twins."

2

"Hey, now, that cannot be the case. How old was Courtney when he died?"

"Eighty-six years summers, my lord."

"Why does everyone always say summers? Why not winters? Anyway, he can't have sired two teenage misses."

"Mr. Courtney married a housemaid, one Annie Plumtree, fifteen years ago. The lady died giving birth to the twins."

"Sad. But see here, is that it? I mean, if I don't want to live in the castle and bring these poxy wenches out, I don't get the inheritance?"

"In a nutshell."

The viscount rose and strolled to the door. "Then I don't want it," he said cheerfully. "Good day to you, Mr. Broome."

"In that case," came the old lawyer's voice as the viscount opened the door, "the inheritance will go to your cousin Basil."

Lord Hunterdon turned around slowly. "You mean Basil Devenham? *Toad* Devenham?"

"Precisely, my lord."

"In that case, I won't say no, but I can't say yes either. Not until I think about it. How long have I got?"

Mr. Broome looked at him maliciously. "We have wasted a considerable amount of time trying to get in touch with you, my lord. I think twenty-four hours would be a fair length of time."

"Oh, very well."

Lord Hunterdon walked pensively out into the sunshine.

How he loathed Basil! Basil Devenham was the same age as the viscount, twenty-eight. The viscount's parents, the Marquess and Marchioness of

Derriwell, had always held Basil up to their errant son as a "good example." Basil was sober and God-fearing. Basil never gambled or went with loose women. Basil was a Good Man. And Basil thought so, too. He had a slimy, unctuous manner. Although he lived just as much a life of leisure as the viscount, he always implied that his days were taken up in study or good works.

The viscount turned in the direction of his club. Surely some of his friends could advise him. When he reached the club in St. James's Street, he found he was in luck. Not one but three of his closest friends were in the coffee room: Lord Charnworth, the Honorable John Trump, and Mr. Paul Jolly. All were about the same age as the viscount, all were unmarried, and all devoted to a life of ease.

"Here comes Beau," Lord Charnworth exclaimed. "He'll cheer us up." Lord Charnworth was a very small gentleman with prematurely white hair he wore frizzed, which, combined with his small features, made him look like a poodle. In fact, there was something doggy about the other two, Mr. Trump being rather like a collie and Mr. Jolly, like a bulldog.

"Can't feel happy," the viscount drawled, dropping elegantly into a chair. "Curst problem on my hands."

"Nancy given you your walking orders, Beau?" Mr. Trump asked sympathetically. Nancy was the viscount's latest mistress.

"No, but I'm beginning to wish *she* would walk away from *me*," the viscount grumbled. "Rapacious, that's what she is. Fact is, I've just been to old Courtney's lawyers, old Mirabel Courtney, distant relative, left me a castle, estates, and a fortune."

"What's so bad about that?" Lord Charnworth asked.

"I've got to live there."

"Still not too bad. Lots of us have to languish in the country for the winter. Nothing wrong with keeping your home in London as a town house."

"Wait, there's worse. This old lecher Courtney married a housemaid fifteen years ago, because, one assumes, he managed to get her pregnant, for she died giving birth to twin girls who are now just fifteen and part of the deal is that I have to find husbands for them. I said I wouldn't accept the inheritance, and then I learned that it would go to Basil Devenham."

"Never!" Mr. Jolly growled. "Sheer waste of money. You've got to go through with it, Beau."

"Don't think I can face it," the viscount remarked.

"But you don't bring these maidens out yourself," Lord Charnworth exclaimed suddenly. "You find a governess for them!"

"Bit old for a governess, surely."

"No, you get one of those dragons who brings misses up to the social mark. Sort of advanced governess. A governess of distinction, that's what you ask for."

"A governess of distinction," the viscount said, turning the phrase over in his mind.

"Sounds a good idea," Mr. Trump said. "Besides, these lawyers can't go running down to wherever it is to make sure you're actually staying there, hey? Go down, see the gels, get the governess, kiss 'em good-bye, pick up the moneybags, back to Town."

"I suppose I could do that. . . ."

"And if it is a really horrible situation," Mr. Trump urged, "why, you can tell the lawyers to let Toad Basil have the lot. Serve him right."

A smile of relief lit up Lord Hunterdon's handsome features. "What a clever lot you are, and you shall have your reward. Champagne, by the bucket!"

A week later—a week of roistering, drinking deep, and gambling hard later—Viscount Hunterdon traveled in the direction of Trelawney Castle. Despite the fact that the hedges were thick and heavy with the leaves and flowers of summer—scarlet poppies, pink and white wild roses, purple and yellow vetch—he felt an odd sense of foreboding which after some thought he put down to indigestion.

The hedges gradually fell back, and he found himself riding across wild heathland. He was driving his own traveling carriage laden down with all the comforts he considered might be necessary to smooth his short stay at the castle. The blue sky above became milky and then darkened to gray, and finally as he came in sight of Trelawney Castle, a threatening black lit with flashes of lightning.

His coachman, who was sitting beside him on the box, crossed himself and said, "Looks like the lair of the devil himself."

And Trelawney Castle did look grim. It was not that it was a castle with battlements and turrets, although there must have been such a building there at one time to give it the name. Rather, it

6

was a Gothic fright built during the eighteenth-century Gothic revival. It had spires and lancet windows and flying buttresses and gargoyles and was, the viscount decided, an architectural mess capable of inflicting damage on the aesthetic soul. He drove past an untenanted lodge through rusty iron gates and up a long, weedy drive bordered on either side by an unkempt jungle of undergrowth.

As he swept the carriage around to stand in front of the main door, he noticed gloomily that all the windows were of stained glass and that the walls were covered in ivy. A flash of lightning struck down, and the horses plunged and reared and then came a tremendous clap of thunder. His servants, the coachman, two grooms, and his valet were all whimpering with terror.

It was like a scene out of a Gothic romance, thought the viscount dismally. He wondered whether there were headless ghosts.

"I hate this place already," he said. "Don't stand there squawking and shaking. It's only a thunderstorm. Announce me!"

A groom approached the door. There was a large brass knocker in the shape of a devil's head. Another flash of lightning, which flickered over the brass door knocker and seemed to make it come to life, followed by another hellish peal of thunder, sent the terrified servant reeling back. The viscount had just climbed down from his carriage in time to receive the frantic embrace of his groom, who was babbling that the door knocker had grinned at him.

"Now, Jiggs," the viscount said, easing off his servant's clutching hands. "You are overset. I will announce myself. Find the kitchens and have some warm ale. Nothing like warm ale for restoring the nerves."

He seized the door knocker and began to bang it heartily.

The door creaked slowly open and a fat, white-faced butler stood there. He was completely bald.

"Welcome home, master," he said in a low, sepulchral voice.

While his servants still crouched behind him, Lord Hunterdon strolled into the hall and looked around. It was fake baronial and in the worst of taste. He began to laugh, a merry, infectious laugh. He turned to his servants. "We have walked straight into the stage of the Haymarket Theatre, have we not, my boys? Enter ghost, stage right."

His servants began to laugh as well while the butler stood by, his fat features showing neither interest nor displeasure.

"Welcome, my lord," the butler said. "My name is Dredwort." The viscount snickered. The butler went to the fireplace and tugged on a massive bell rope beside it. "The staff will wish to pay their respects, my lord."

The staff came filing into the gloomy hall and formed a line before the viscount. He walked down the line which started with the housekeeper and ended with the lamp boy. It was, however, not a large enough staff of servants for such a place, thought the viscount. The men's livery was old-fashioned and threadbare and the women's gowns were worn and darned.

The viscount correctly judged from the poor livery and the state of the grounds that the late Mr. Courtney had been something of a miser.

"And where are the Misses Amanda and Clarissa?" he asked.

"They have retired for the night," Dredwort said, "and beg to be excused."

"Well, I want to meet them," the viscount snapped. "It ain't that late. Fetch them here. May as well get it over with. Show me to some comfortable room and bring me brandy."

"Mr. Courtney always used the library in the evenings, and I have had a fire lit there."

"Hey, Dredwort, you ain't going to turn out to be one of those pesky retainers who want everything to remain the same, I hope. Show the way."

The library was a gloomy place, the furniture heavy and Jacobean. A small fire burned in a cavernous fireplace big enough to roast an ox. "Not short of wood, are we?" the viscount demanded. "Throw a few trees in here, bring the brandy, and let me get my introduction to the girls over and done with."

The butler inclined his head and withdrew. The viscount paced up and down. He did not like Trelawney Castle, he did not like the gloomy atmosphere, and above all, he did not like this new feeling of responsibility.

The door opened and he turned about. "Miss Amanda and Miss Clarissa," Dredwort announced.

The viscount looked at the twins, and the twins, holding hands, stared back. "Got a governess?" he asked.

"No, my lord," they chorused.

The viscount crossed to a writing desk in the far corner. "Well, you're getting one now."

* * *

Two days later, in an uncomfortable house situated at the end of a damp little village called Gunshott, sat Miss Jean Morrison, enjoying a moment's peace from the hectoring sound of her aunt's voice.

Jean felt her young life had been governed by a succession of bullies. Her mother had died when Jean was very young. Her father, a colonel in a Scottish regiment, had sold out and returned to his mountain home to oversee the bringing up of his daughter. To that end he had hired a formidable governess and had given her free rein. The governess, Miss Tiggs, an Englishwoman, had bullied Jean unmercifully. When the colonel died a year before, Jean had sacked the governess with great pleasure, and, because she had hardly any money, had gone to live with an aunt in Edinburgh, in the hope that the aunt would bring her out at the Edinburgh assemblies and find her a husband. But the aunt, Mrs. Macleod, had wanted Jean only as a companion, and an overworked one at that. Finding she had jumped out of the frying pan into the fire, Jean had written to another aunt, Mrs. Delmar-Richardson in Dorset and begged asylum.

To her delight, she received a courteous letter assuring her of a welcome. With some of the little money she had left, she had taken the long road south, dreaming of happiness. But Mrs. Delmar-Richardson was another bully of the chilly grande-dame kind. Jean quickly realized she was expected to wait on the lady hand and foot, to read to her, to walk behind her, carrying her shawl, to play the piano for her, and any number of tiresome tasks that kept her anchored to Mrs. Delmar-Richardson's side.

Besides, Mrs. Delmar-Richardson was ugly, and Jean's one weakness was a craving for beauty. She herself had long given up any hope of growing into beauty. At the age of twenty, she had dark red hair, a terrible thing for any lady to have, green eyes, pale, almost translucent skin, and a neat figure.

Her aunt had mercifully drunk too much during the afternoon and had retired to her bed. Jean, who knew there were no novels allowed in the house, settled down instead to read the local papers. That was how she came across the viscount's advertisement. She read it several times. A governess of distinction was wanted to train two young misses in the social arts. Jean herself had been trained in the social arts in the remote Highlands of Scotland just as if she were about to make her debut at Almack's Assembly Rooms in London. Her heart began to beat hard, and hope, dormant for some time, sprang anew. One side of Jean's mind was down-to-earth and practical, but the other side dreamed of romance. The advertisement stated clearly that all applicants were to apply in writing. Jean quickly decided that if she went there in person, she might secure the job. She put on her bonnet and cloak, went down into the village, asked the road to Trelawney Castle, and learned it was only ten miles away.

Without saying a word to her aunt, she rose early the following morning, carrying only a small trunk, optimistically planning to send the viscount's servants to collect the rest of her belongings which she had left packed in her bedroom. If she did not get the position—well, that did not even bear thinking of. Her hopes high, she set out on foot under a gray and lowering sky. Trelawney Castle, she had learned, was on the coast. Lord Hunterdon had recently inherited it. He was unmarried.

Dreams about an unmarried viscount and a castle happily engaged Jean's thoughts. He would be Byronic and brooding, tortured and miserable, pacing the battlements with a black cloak wrapped around his manly shoulders. He would soften under her influence until one day he would seize her in his arms and cry, "Be mine, Jean Morrison!"

Jean finally reached the deserted lodge and rusty gates. It was all very depressing. She had heard Mr. Courtney was rich, and surely a viscount was rich. Jean had been brought up on the lines of a penny saved is a penny earned, and she had been looking forward to luxurious surroundings.

When she came in sight of the house, her heart sank. This was no romantic castle. Instead, it was a Gothic monstrosity, dark and sinister.

All sorts of doubts rushed into her head. She did not have any references. The impertinence of her action took her breath away. But then, behind her was her aunt. Better at least try.

She seized the knocker and gave it a good bang, wondering what sort of household put a brass devil's head on its main door as a knocker.

The door creaked opened and Dredwort stared down at her.

Jean tremulously presented one of her cards which had the Highland address scored out and then the Edinburgh address scored out and the Gunshott address penciled in.

"I am come," she said in a shaky voice, "in answer to Lord Hunterdon's advertisement."

Dredwort frowned. He knew of no advertisement. Then he remembered a footman had been sent to deliver a letter to the local newspaper offices. His eyes ranged from her plain bonnet to her buckled shoes. All were of good quality.

"Advertisement for what, miss?"

"Governess, to be sure," Jean said tartly. "It is beginning to rain. Pray allow me to step inside."

"I will inform his lordship," Dredwort said coldly. "Wait here."

So Jean waited with her battered trunk at her feet in the great hall, looking in amazement at the fake medieval flags, the suits of armor, the general air of damp and neglect.

The great mansion was very quiet. Jean could not understand it. She opened her cloak and squinted down at the watch pinned to her bosom. Ten o'clock. The servants should have been in evidence, working about. Perhaps they rose very early indeed to complete their duties.

After half an hour Dredwort came slowly down the dim wooden staircase. "Follow me," he said in a hollow voice.

Jean left her trunk in the hall and walked up the stairs after the butler. Various old paintings, so dark and dirty that it was almost impossible to make out what they were supposed to be, hung on the walls. The staircase was uncarpeted and not very clean.

"The drawing room," Dredwort intoned, throwing open a pair of double doors. "Wait here for his lordship."

Jean felt a lump rising to her throat. Here was neither elegance nor comfort. The room was cold. The furniture was musty and dusty, as were the curtains. An old game bag lay in one corner and a pile of fishing rods in another.

She began to wonder again about this future employer. He could not be either handsome or Byronic. No one with the slightest sensitivity could live in a place like this. He was probably the sort of man who enjoyed cockfights and never washed.

A tear rolled down her cheek, followed by another, and she fumbled in her pocket for a handkerchief.

"Take mine," said a masculine voice, and Jean looked up at the viscount through a blur of tears.

"Thank you." She firmly wiped her eyes and stood up and curtsied, and then looked up into the face of the most handsome man she had ever seen. Even in this gloomy room his hair shone like gold, his eyes were as blue as the summer sea, and his lightly tanned skin without a single flaw. He was wrapped in a glorious Oriental dressing gown, and he smelled faintly of lavender water and soap.

"Why are you crying?" His voice was light and pleasant.

"I was not really crying," Jean lied. "Something must have got in my eye."

"Probably the horrors surrounding you," the viscount said sympathetically. "Coffee is what you need. Strong coffee with a dash of something in it." He tugged the dusty bell rope, which came away in his hand. "Tcha!" he said in disgust. He opened the door and found himself face-to-face with Dredwort.

"Get coffee, brandy, biscuits," the viscount snapped. "At the double."

He returned to the drawing room and sat down. "So this is the drawing room," he said, looking about him. "Dear me. Sit down, Miss . . . ?"

"Morrison. Jean Morrison."

"And you are come in answer to my advertisement, in which I clearly stated applications had to be made in writing?"

"Yes, my lord. I live quite nearby and I thought it easier to call in person."

He held out a white hand. "References."

"I have not any."

"Then why should I employ you? Good heavens, the magnitude of the task demands experience."

Jean looked at him resolutely. She did not have much hope, but she would fight to stay with this god. "I am very well schooled, my lord, in all the social arts." She talked about her upbringing and why she was so eager to escape from her aunt.

He looked at her sympathetically. "Had a rotten life," he commented. "Here is the coffee. Put it down on that table next to Miss Morrison, Dredwort, and leave us."

When the door had closed behind the butler, the viscount said easily, "Now, before you pour that coffee, take off your cloak and bonnet and make yourself comfortable."

He intended to send her on her way as soon as she had drunk something. He had no intention of hiring a young and inexperienced girl.

Jean Morrison obediently swung her cloak from her shoulders and removed her bonnet. The viscount bit back an exclamation. Her hair was red, bright shining red, that darkish Highland color that often seems to have purple lights in it.

Jean saw him staring at it and flushed miserably. Neither aunt had let her cut it, and it was now tumbling down her back. "I am willing to dye it, my lord."

"No, sacrilege," he said faintly, looking in a bemused way at all the waves and curls.

He got up, poured a cup of coffee, and added a strong measure of brandy to it. Jean took it doubtfully. "I have never drunk spirits before, my lord." She suddenly smiled, a warm, blinding smile. "But I am willing to try."

The viscount looked around the bleak room and then back to the glowing little figure of this would-be governess. She'd brighten up the place, he thought. Seemed sensible enough. Still . . .

"There's a piano over there," he said. "Do you play?"

"Yes, my lord."

"Then play me something."

The brandy had gone to Jean's head, and she felt elated and not at all like her usual dull self. She went confidently to the piano and began to play a Haydn sonata, her fingers rippling competently over the keys while the viscount leaned back in his chair. Odd, how a woman at the piano could suddenly make this miserable heap seem like a home, he thought.

When she had finished, he quizzed her about her education and learned to his surprise that she could read Latin and Greek and had a thorough knowledge of what was referred to as the "masculine sciences," namely mathematics, physics, and chemistry. She then went on to explain that she also knew how to behave in the ballroom, at the dinner table, how to accept or repulse compliments, how to cut people dead, and how to make calls.

He made up his mind. "I see no reason why you should not be put on trial. But before *you* make up your mind, you had best meet your charges."

He went to the door. As he expected, Dredwort was standing outside, where he had been listening to every word. "Fetch the young ladies here," he ordered, "and bring me the account books." The viscount did not know how much to pay this governess, but he had learned that the twins had had governesses in the past and so that should give him some indication of what to pay Miss Morrison.

Jean waited nervously to meet her new charges. They would, she thought, be very aristocratic, perhaps beautiful. But they were not so very far from her own age and perhaps they could all be friends.

She drank her coffee and brandy in silence while the account books were brought in and the viscount went through them.

"This is ridiculous. Come here, Miss Morrison." Jean went and stood behind him as he ran a long finger down the page. "Have you ever seen such miserable wages? No wonder the servants are not efficient. Dredwort! I know you are listening outside. Come in!"

He handed the account books to the butler. "Double all the wages of the staff immediately and order new livery for the men and dresses for the women."

A smile dawned on the butler's fat white face. It creased up until his whole face glowed. "Oh, yes, my lord. Thank you, my lord."

"But everything has to sparkle, mind you. Rotten summer. Fires in all the rooms."

"Why is there no one in the lodge?" Jean asked, emboldened by brandy and success.

"Mr. Courtney turned them out. Mr. Hannay and his family."

"And where are they now?"

"In the workhouse, my lord."

"This is quite dreadful. Get them out of the workhouse as soon as possible. Get builders or whatever you need to repair the place and the gates. I have an agent, do I not?"

"Mr. Peterman over at St. Giles."

"Get him. I want him now."

"Very good, my lord."

"Wicked old man," the viscount said, meaning Mr. Courtney. He suddenly pasted a strained smile on his face. "Why, here are the girls. Girls, make your curtsy to Miss Morrison, your new governess."

Jean looked at the twins and her heart sank. They were both small and fat with black greasy hair and malicious little black eyes. Their dresses were dirty and they smelled abominable.

They curtsied and then stood hand in hand, staring at her. "The one with the eyebrows is Amanda," the viscount said, and Amanda did indeed have black eyebrows across her brow in a straight bar. "T'other is Clarissa."

"Your hair is awfully red," Clarissa said. Her voice had a strong country accent.

"Your first lesson," Jean said firmly, "is not to make personal comments. Perhaps, my lord, the girls will show me the schoolroom while one of your servants fetches my belongings from my aunt. She is Mrs. Delmar-Richardson of Peartrees, Gunshott."

"That will be done," the viscount said. "The housekeeper is Mrs. Moody. I will send her to you and she will show you to your quarters. Girls, take Miss Morrison to the schoolroom."

The girls trudged out and Jean followed them. They led her up to the top of the house. The schoolroom had a little-used look. It was cold and dusty. It contained a teacher's desk and two pupils' desks.

"We may as well begin by getting to know each other," Jean said. "Sit down."

"Enjoy yourself while you can," Clarissa said. "We'll soon get rid of you."

Jean ignored that. She opened the lid of her desk and saw that it contained sheets of paper, pens, and ink. She selected two steel pens, a bottle of ink, and two sheets of paper.

"Now," she said, placing everything in front of them, "you will both begin by starting to write, 'A lady should never be rude.' "

They stared at her in dumb insolence.

But Jean Morrison was full of unaccustomed brandy and Jean Morrison was suddenly determined to fight every inch of the way to stay with the golden viscount. She saw a cane standing in the corner of the room. She picked it up and brought it down with a crash across Amanda's desk. Green eyes blazing, Jean Morrison ordered, "Write!"

Chapter Two

THERE WAS A SHOCKED SILENCE in the schoolroom. Then the girls dipped their pens in the ink bottle and began to write, slowly and painfully. Jean read, "A lady shude never be rood."

She put down the cane, ashamed of her own outburst. Poor girls. Poor semiliterate girls. "No, no," she said gently. "I will write it correctly for you and you may copy it." In firm copperplate she wrote down the phrase just as the housekeeper came into the room. "Miss Morrison," Mrs. Moody said, "I am come to show you to your room."

"Continue writing, girls," Jean ordered. "Fifty times. That one sentence."

Mrs. Moody was delighted with this new governess. Jean thought of herself as plain and would have been startled to know that the servants put down their sudden increase in good fortune to the effect of her feminine charms on the viscount. As she followed the housekeeper downstairs and along a corridor on the second floor, Jean could hear the house coming to life. The servants were all hard at work.

She was shown into a large bedchamber with a high bed, high because it had five mattresses, four of horsehair and straw topped with a feather one. The bedroom had obviously just been cleaned and a fire was burning in the fireplace. Fresh jugs of water had been placed on the toilet table.

"We hope you will be very happy here," Mrs. Moody said. "But be warned, miss, them hellions upstairs have put rout to I dunno how many governesses."

"They are unfortunate, that is all," Jean said. "What was old Mr. Courtney like?"

"A bit strange," the housekeeper said cautiously. "Got tighter and tighter with money."

"He must keep a generous table, however," Jean said. "The girls are too fat."

"Well, I'm blessed if I know where they get the money from, and that's a fact," the housekeeper said. "Always stuffing themselves with chocolates and sugarplums. But it wasn't from any feeding they got from old Mr. Courtney."

Jean picked up her trunk and put it on the bed. "I will just leave my clothes out on the bed, Mrs. Moody. I do not want to leave my charges alone too long."

"I'll gladly send the maids up to put everything away for you."

"That will not be necessary." Jean did not want the servants to see how plain and unfashionable her wardrobe was. She dismissed the housekeeper, quickly spread her small stock of clothes out on the bed, and arranged her brush and comb on the toilet table.

Then she went back to the schoolroom. It was empty. The girls had written only three blotted lines each. She rang the bell and told a footman to send the servants to look for them. Then she waited a half hour before deciding to go to her room and put her clothes away. The rest of her things should be arriving shortly.

She opened the door of her room and then stood, shocked, on the threshold. All her clothes had been cut and slashed and left in ribbons on the bed. Her brush was burning merrily in the fireplace along with what she gathered was the remains of her comb.

She went to a chair by the window, sat down, and clasped her knees to stop them from trembling. If she told the viscount, he would pay her for the damage and then he would probably dismiss her, as she could not maintain discipline—which was just what the twins wanted.

Jean thought of the golden viscount and of the kind way he had given her his handkerchief. She still had it. She took it out and spread it on her lap, her fingers caressing the monogram.

No, she thought. She was not going to be trounced by that couple of fiends. She carefully packed the ruined clothes back into the trunk and climbed up to the schoolroom, carrying it.

The twins were sitting at their desks, writing busily. Jean rang the bell and asked for a workbasket to be brought to the schoolroom.

The twins wrote on, heads down, the picture of innocence.

"Now," Jean said grimly, "we will have a lesson in sewing. Put aside your writing and bring your chairs next to me. It is of no use protesting your innocence. You wrecked my clothes and you will repair them."

She drew out two of the slashed dresses. "One each. You will repair the slashes with neat stitches.

Your work will be ripped out and you will start again if it is not neat enough. Begin."

Clarissa got up, walked over to Jean, and slapped her full across the face while Amanda cheered. Jean slapped Clarissa back with all her force.

"You bitch!" Clarissa said with a tinge of admiration in her voice.

"Begin!" Jean ordered, picking up the cane which she had no intention of using except in self-defense.

They stitched and stitched, clumsy, painful stitches. Jean duly ripped them out and set the twins to the task again. After they had been working for two hours, Jean looked out of the window and saw the sun was shining.

"We will go for a walk," she announced, "and then we will resume again on our return. Fetch your cloaks and bonnets."

Soon all were walking away from the house, Jean behind and the twins in front, their heads together, whispering, and occasionally looking back at her. Jean was determined to enjoy the sudden good weather. They walked through the gardens at the back of the house and down to a curve of white sandy beach. Great glassy waves curled and broke on the shore. "This is beautiful," Jean said.

"I prefer Peter's Tarn, inland. It's more beautiful," Amanda volunteered.

Glad of some sign of aesthetic appreciation from one of these horrible girls, Jean asked eagerly, "Is it far? Could you take me there?"

"Not far," Amanda said laconically, and the twins turned inland. After a mile they came to the tarn, or small lake. It was almost a complete circle and as smooth as a mirror. Two weeping willows dipped their long branches into the water. The air was still and warm and sweet. Jean stood on a flat rock overhanging the water and looked down.

"It is indeed so very beautiful," she said. "How deep is it, do you think?"

"Have a closer look and you'll find out," Amanda said from behind her.

And then with one almighty push, she sent Jean flying over the edge and into the water.

Arm in arm Amanda and Clarissa strolled off, deaf to the cries for help that were coming from the tarn.

"That's got rid of her," Amanda said. "Know'd it wouldn't take long. Silly bitch."

"Had a good bit o' spirit, though," Clarissa pointed out. "Think her'll drown?"

"Perhaps, perhaps not."

The viscount looked appalled at the little trunkful of slashed clothes Mrs. Moody had brought down from the schoolroom. "I'm telling you, my lord," Mrs. Moody said, "them's that governess's clothes what she had placed on the bed of her room. Those fiends must have cut them up. Did Miss Morrison say nothing to you of it?"

"No, Mrs. Moody. She will be recompensed, of course. Where is she now?"

"Well, that's the trouble, my lord. John, the second footman, said as how he had seen her go out for a walk with Miss Amanda and Miss Clarissa. Now, them other governesses, they usually took one of the men along for protection."

"From footpads?"

"No, my lord, from the Courtney girls."

"But didn't old Mr. Courtney know what was going on?"

"He was a bit senile, my lord, and wouldn't hear a word against his daughters. Don't think they was his, but you couldn't tell him that." Mrs. Moody leaned one of her broad hips against a table and prepared for a comfortable gossip.

"No, I don't see how they could be unless he was able to father them at the age of seventy-one, although that is not beyond the bounds of possibility. But we must go to look for Miss Morrison."

He hurried down the stairs and out onto the grounds. And then he saw the twins walking slowly toward the house. They were arm in arm and highly pleased about something.

He ran toward them. "Where is Miss Morrison?"

Amanda gave him a slow smile. "Reckon as how her's gone for a swim."

Dread clutched at his throat. "Where?"

"Peter's Tarn," Clarissa volunteered.

He looked at their fat white faces in horror. "You pushed her in!"

"Her fell," Clarissa protested while Amanda stifled a snort of laughter.

"If you have killed her, then you will both hang and I shall see to it personally," the viscount said. He was by now surrounded by a ring of listening servants.

"Take these girls to the schoolroom and lock them in," he ordered. "You men, come with me and show me where this tarn is."

The viscount and a group of servants set off at a run. "Please God she is still alive," the viscount prayed. "This is too much. Damn the money and damn the inheritance. Basil is welcome to it."

And then, in the distance, he saw a small figure, striding along, the sun glinting on her red hair.

He let out a long sigh of pure relief. Jean Morrison!

She came up to him and smiled in a composed way, although her face was very white and her clothes dripping wet. "Thank God you were able to swim," he said.

Jean half closed her eyes as she remembered those terrifying few moments when she thought she would drown. "No," she said evenly, "I am not able to swim. I was able to grasp the branches of a willow tree overhanging the water and pull myself out. But the so-charming Misses Courtney were not to know that."

"No, they were not. I will send for the magistrate if you wish and have them charged with attempted murder."

Jean had planned, as she walked back, to tell him that she was leaving. But he stood there before her, his hat in his hand, his blue eyes full of concern, and the sunlight glinting in his thick fair curls, and her heart turned over.

"We will see," she said quietly. "I am on trial, but they are on trial with me. Something may yet be done with them."

He courteously held out his arm and she gratefully took it. The servants following, they made their way back to the castle. "Furthermore," the viscount said, "they ruined your dresses. Oh, yes, Mrs. Moody told me. You will be paid handsomely for them."

"Thank you, my lord. Has Mrs. Delmar-Richardson sent my belongings?"

"Yes, and sent me a stern note. She is to call."

"Oh, dear, I have had enough to face today," Jean mourned. "As to dresses, perhaps it would be a good idea to hire a seamstress. I will take the girls to the nearest town tomorrow and choose material for myself and for them. Pretty dresses are such a civilizing influence."

"As you will. But take two of the strongest servants with you."

"Perhaps the young ladies might find their appearance improved by the services of a lady's maid . . . a very strong and muscular lady's maid."

"That they shall have. You know, Miss Morrison, I do not need to be troubled with the Misses Courtney or the castle and lands. I can tell the lawyers I don't want any of it and it will all go to Toad Basil!"

"And who is Toad Basil?"

"Basil Devenham, my cousin."

"And would Basil Devenham do something for these poor servants and for tenants such as the lodge-keeper and his family who were driven off to the workhouse?"

"No, he'd probably find a few more to impoverish."

"Well, then, it is not as if it is too onerous a task. You have me to take care of the twins, you need a good agent to cope with everything else. A good agent would leave you free to do as you wished."

"You have the right of it. I miss the fun of London. I miss—" He bit his lip. He had been about to mention Nancy. He could never mention his mistress to such a lady as Miss Morrison, or, indeed, he thought ruefully, to any lady.

"There is, however, something else."

"Yes, Miss Morrison?"

"The Misses Courtney do not seem to have been taught the difference between right and wrong. I think the vicar should call on them and give them some religious instruction. In pushing me into the water, they acted on spiteful impulse, but they did not mean to murder me, of that I am sure."

"I will try, but I cannot help feeling a prison chaplain might be more in their line. The only thing to lighten my gloom is that I find Mr. Courtney has built up an excellent cellar. When you have changed, join me for a glass of claret."

Jean's heart rose and then fell again. He was treating her with the same easy camaraderie as he probably treated his masculine friends.

Before she parted from him in the hall, he said, "Those brats are locked in the schoolroom. Leave them there until I think what best to say to them and join me in the drawing room . . . no, make it the library. The drawing room is depressing."

Jean went upstairs, realizing she had not eaten all day. She dressed and changed and then, before she went downstairs, she asked to be taken to the twins' bedchamber. In it she discovered boxes of chocolates, sweet biscuits, and sugarplums. She told the servants to take them all down to the kitchens and share them among the rest of the staff.

Then with a final pat to her hair she went down to the library.

The viscount poured her a glass of claret. He had a vague feeling that he should not be on such familiar terms with a governess, but he felt the need of someone to talk to. "The agent, a Josiah Peterman, is calling shortly. I have been glancing through the estate books. The rents are too high. I want to know what this bloodsucker was about."

Jean sipped her claret. "Perhaps he was simply acting under Mr. Courtney's instructions."

"Mr. Peterman," Dredwort announced.

A small, old white-haired man came into the room.

"Well, Peterman," the viscount said, "what have you to say for yourself? I've been going through the books, and I don't like the look of the rents at all."

"My lord," the old man said miserably, "I cannot think it possible to extract any more."

"I am not telling you to extract more, man, I'm telling you to extract less."

"But Mr. Courtney was most insistent, most insistent. He said I would lose my job if I did not go on raising the rents."

The viscount clutched his fair curls. "Listen, I am not Courtney. We will ride out tomorrow and see the tenants. Repairs must be made where repairs are needed. No more rent to be paid until they come about. Any more apart from the lodgekeeper in the workhouse?"

"Oh, yes, my lord."

"Then get them all out and put them back. I was going to fire you, Peterman, but I see you have been simply saving your own skin. Be here at nine in the morning and we will start making reparation."

"Oh, my lord, this is a happy day. I call down the blessings of all the angels on—"

"Don't start preaching at me. You make my head ache. Off with you, and we will arrange everything in the morning. And then hire painters and builders and decorators and let us put some life into this mausoleum!"

Jean, who had been thinking her master was a saint, quickly changed her mind when the agent had left and he said, "How all this bores me! I'll be glad when it's over and I can get back to Town and kick up my heels."

"Mrs. Delmar-Richardson," Dredwort intoned.

Jean's aunt sailed in. Her cold glance at the two, sitting companionably drinking claret, seemed to realize her worst fears.

"So!" she said.

Jean found to her fury that she was blushing. She admired the viscount, who got to his feet, made a brief bow, and then politely waited for more.

"I am come!" Mrs. Delmar-Richardson declared.

"Do you usually stand in doorways making obvious statements?" asked the viscount with interest.

Mrs. Delmar-Richardson threw back her head. "I am come to remove my niece from a den of iniquity."

Suddenly the viscount's merry, easygoing manner changed. "Explain your impertinence, madam," he said frostily.

"I find my niece has fled a respectable home to join the demimonde."

"I never did like all this country living," the viscount said with a sigh. He sat down again and took up his glass. "Inbreeding, bad drainage, damp houses—all makes people totty-headed."

Jean found her voice. "Go away, Aunt."

"And leave you to bring shame on the family? Never!"

"Dredwort!" the viscount shouted, and when the bald butler oiled into the room, he added, "This lady is leaving, and very quickly, too, if you take my meaning."

"Certainly, my lord. This way, madam."

"You have not heard the last from me," Mrs. Delmar-Richardson declared.

"I do sincerely hope so," the viscount said equably. "Close the door, Dredwort, there is a dreadful draft."

"Oh, dear," Jean said when the door was closed firmly behind her enraged aunt, "now I have really burnt my boats."

The viscount looked at her in consternation. "You mean I am all you have got now?"

"Yes, my lord."

"I should have thought of that before I sent her packing," he said ruefully. "As if those hellcats upstairs weren't enough."

Jean winced.

He rose to his feet. "Time I had a talk to them. Go and change for dinner. We eat in an hour."

The viscount went up the stairs to the schoolroom followed by Dredwort, who produced a key and unlocked the door.

"Now, look here, you two," the viscount said, eyeing the twins with disfavor, "I haven't sent for the magistrate . . . yet. But if you do not behave, if you do not do everything Miss Morrison tells you to do, then I will see you are both charged with attempted murder."

"You wouldn't,"Amanda gasped.

"Yes, I would, and gladly. You mean nothing to me. I find you both coarse, common, and dangerous. Nonetheless, you will present yourself at dinner." He wrinkled his nose fastidiously. "Dredwort, two baths up to their bedchamber and the stoutest housemaids to wash them. If they try to abuse or hit or molest the servants in any way, the servants have my permission to hit back."

Amanda and Clarissa began to realize their reign of terror was over. Their father had not allowed any of his servants even to complain about them.

Soon both were being ruthlessly scrubbed by womenservants from top to toe.

Jean heard the screams and put her hands quickly over her ears. She assumed the girls were being beaten. She should have been glad of it, but she was not. She herself had been beaten regularly in her youth and she knew it did nothing to improve the spirit.

She was glad when the sounds of shouting and weeping died away. With shaking fingers she opened her trunks, which had arrived from her aunt's house, took out a plain gray silk gown, and looked at it ruefully. Jean had always longed for more fashionable clothes. She wondered whether she could bring herself to face the twins again that day and then decided against it. She and the viscount would be alone at dinner, for the twins would surely take their meals in the schoolroom.

She went down to the library.

She stopped in the doorway in consternation. Clarissa and Amanda were there, both wearing clean muslin gowns. Their black hair was still damp from the bath. The twins rose and curtsied to her and said meekly in chorus, "Good evening, Miss Morrison."

"Good evening," Jean replied faintly as she walked into the room. Amanda said, "We are both mortal sorry we pushed you in. We never thought for a moment you'd any chance o' being drownded. We're oh so very sorry and may God strike us dead if we ain't telling the truth."

Clarissa thought of that humiliating bath, and tears of rage coursed down her fat cheeks.

"There now," Jean said, mollified, relieved, and

surprised all at once, "we will say no more about it."

"Unless," the viscount added sotto voce, "you give me reason to remember it."

Dinner was a surprisingly pleasant affair, although the dining room proved to be like the other rooms in the house, dark and dismal. The food was plain but well cooked. The viscount talked of plays and parties and balls in London, and the only thing that marred the evening for Jean was the trace of wistfulness in his voice.

"Do you have many friends in London?" Amanda asked suddenly.

"Yes, I am fortunate. I have three in particular, bachelor friends. There's Mr. John Trump, Mr. Paul Jolly, and Lord Charnworth. We usually meet up at White's. Oh, that I were there now."

Jean felt sad. But why should such an elegant aristocrat enjoy being immured in the country and in such company?

All were tired, and Jean was relieved when she was allowed to retire immediately after dinner. The viscount had promised her a generous sum of money to take the girls shopping in St. Giles, the nearest town. Two grooms were to accompany her, and also the underhousekeeper, a thin, wiry woman called Mrs. Pewsey. Jean thought it quite mad that the first thing she did when introduced to Mrs. Pewsey was to check that lady's figure for signs of physical strength. But someone strong was needed to control the girls in case they got into mischief.

Amanda and Clarissa went up to their bedchamber and held a council of war. "I have an idea," Amanda said. "Get rid o' him, and it'll be easy to deal with her."

"How?"

"He's bored. He's a dilly ... dilly ... you know, a sort of fop, pining for the pleasures of London. We can write to those friends o' his, supposed to be from him, and invite them down. He'll be too taken up with them to keep an eye on us."

"Fool," Clarissa sneered. "How can we write such a letter?"

"Gully Thomson," Amanda retorted triumphantly.

Clarissa let out a long, slow breath of admiration. Gully Thomson lived in St. Giles. He was usually drunk and was reported to be a gentleman who had come down in the world. He gained money for drink by writing letters for the illiterate section of the town's population.

"We'll never get a chance to get away from her tomorrow," Clarissa pointed out.

"So we'll go tonight."

It was a six-mile walk to St. Giles, but there was a bright moon and the girls were buoyed up by a feeling that they were about to get even with their persecutors.

They found Gully Thomson in his usual spot, the corner of the taproom of The Eagle. The tavern on the outskirts of the town was a low place, full of smugglers and other criminals. The twins were well known. They often called on Gully and so nobody even bothered to turn and look at them as they would have done in a more respectable inn if two young ladies had walked into the tap.

Amanda was delighted to find that Gully was sober enough to understand what was being asked. "There's a sovereign in it if you do it right," she said. "This Lord Hunterdon, Viscount Hunterdon, has three friends who go to White's. We wants a letter to them gentlemen, telling them that he's pining for a bit of fun and inviting them all down, and ask them to bring some women. That'll put that Scotch whore's nose out o' joint."

Gully lifted his traveling writing desk onto the table. He always had it with him in the hope of earning money.

He had done work for Amanda only six months before. Amanda had been smitten by a handsome young gentleman staying at The Crown, a respectable posting house in St. Giles. Gully had written a beautiful letter for her, asking this gentleman to meet her. The letter had been so good that the gentleman had turned up. But unfortunately, one look at little fat Amanda and her beetling eyebrows had made him take to his heels.

"I haven't got paper of good enough quality," he said. The enterprising Amanda opened a newspaper she was carrying, which held several sheets of parchment, a seal, a draft copy of that advertisement for a governess that the viscount had sent to the newspaper, and a copy of his signature. "I took these from the library," she said. "I can put them back tonight."

"Names of friends?" Gully asked. He was a tall, thin man with sparse brown hair that hung in greasy locks about his face. His clothes were shabby and stained with snuff and wine, but his voice was mellow and pleasant, the voice of the gentleman he used to be.

"Lord Charnworth, Mr. Paul Jolly, and Mr. John Trump," Clarissa said promptly. She had the better memory of the two. "That will be the Honorable

John Trump," Gully said knowledgeably, for he read the social columns.

He bent his head and got to work, beginning, "My dear friends." In it, he wrote on behalf of the viscount that he, the viscount, was dying of boredom and longing for some jolly female company as well as the pleasure of seeing his friends again.

Amanda scrutinized the letter carefully when he had finished, asking him to read out and explain the words she could not understand.

"I hear you've got a new governess," Gully said. "Why don't you both learn to read and write properly? You're supposed to be ladies, and yet your dress and manner is that of peasants."

"Watch your tongue or you don't get paid," Amanda snapped.

"Watch your own or you don't get this letter," Gully said.

It was finally agreed that Gully, given some extra money, should send the letter express by the mail coach in the morning. Then the sisters walked off.

"What'll we do to her tomorrow?" Clarissa asked.

"Nothing. Hunterdon is quite likely to get us sent to prison. We do what she asks. We behave like model misses and then we wait and we watch. Come on! Race you home!"

The next day, the viscount found he was becoming more bored and more irritable. Getting grateful families out of the workhouse and putting them back in their homes should have given him a warm feeling of philanthropy, but it did not. He felt he was performing a long, tiresome series of duties. The only thing that gave him any slight pleasure as he passed money freely to the poor was that old Mr. Courtney would have been furious. The reason that the viscount passed that long day in ordering repairs to roofs and windows, hedges and walls was a feeling that the sooner it was all done, the sooner he could return to London and enjoy himself.

"Yes, yes," he said testily as a weeping woman along with her husband and five children were reinstated in their cottage, "I am sure you are very grateful, but you must not kiss my hand. I do not like it. Strive for some dignity, please. You are only being returned to your home." He pushed open the low door of the cottage. "Where is your furniture?" he asked, looking around.

"The bailiffs took it, my lord," the man said.

"Of all the miserable old scroungers, Mr. Courtney was the worst. You must have somewhere to sit. Not a pot to cook anything in." He walked back outside and faced the squad of outdoor servants and workmen who had been following him from cottage to cottage. "The roof needs repair," the viscount said, squinting up at it. "I want basic foodstuffs for the kitchen here and the necessary pots and pans. I need beds and bedding and furniture. The castle is full of horrible stuff just lying there. Take what you need out of the guest bedrooms and the kitchens and bring it all over on the cart. In fact, you had better load up several carts because we have so many places to restore to good order. You will all be working well after sundown and so you will all get extra wages if you do your work well. Mr. Peterman, this family is Trent, is it not? Very well, take a note. Trent. Everything for the household needed. Ask Mrs. Moody to help you. Where is the next hovel on the itinerary?"

"Becket's farm, half a mile away. We took Becket and his family from the workhouse."

"So because of Mr. Courtney's evil parsimony, one good farm has been lying fallow? Tcha! On we go. Will this day never end?"

And so the golden viscount, who seemed like an angel to families who were being restored to their homes, brushed aside all gratitude. All day long, carts rumbled along the roads from the castle, bearing furniture, food, and pots and pans. "There will be nothing left in the castle," Mr. Peterman pleaded.

"Good," the viscount said. "Nasty, gloomy stuff. Great chance to get rid of the lot of it."

And so the workmen labored busily. A huge four-poster with silk hangings was delivered to the Trents. The posts had to be sawed down so that it would fit into the tiny cottage bedchamber, but the grateful Mrs. Trent took the brocaded silk hangings and subsequently the whole Trent family were to be seen on Sunday, finely dressed in clothes of silk brocade.

Finally, the viscount ended up at the farthest-flung farm on his estate. To his surprise, it appeared prosperous, and the farmer, Mr. Tulley, and his family looked well fed.

Pouring ale, Mr. Tulley said that he had managed to keep the farm at a reasonable rent by threatening to kill Mr. Courtney if he raised it. "He believed me, too," the farmer said with a grin.

"But the old skinflint would have made even more money," the viscount pointed out, "if he had made the farms pay."

"He liked humiliating people," Mr. Tulley said.

"Like meat and drink it was to him at the end. Liked that better than money."

The viscount finished his ale and, being offered more, gratefully accepted it. The farmhouse parlor was pretty and bright with flowers. He was reluctant to return to his own gloomy home. For the first time that long day, he remembered Jean Morrison and wondered how she fared in St. Giles.

Jean, to her amazement, had had a successful day. The girls were quiet and obedient. She chose bolts of cloth for dresses for them and for herself. She had meant to choose cloth for gowns that would be suitable for a governess, but the dark little mercers contained an amazing supply of the best French silks and India muslins, and Jean lost her head and shopped for herself as if she were about to make her debut in London.

On her return, she found a dressmaker waiting for her, hired by Mrs. Moody on orders from the viscount. Jean had bought patterns, and together, she and the dressmaker, sitting on the floor of the drawing room that had inexplicably lost all its furniture, planned new wardrobes.

Then dinner was served to her in the dining room, which was still furnished, but the viscount did not arrive. Jean was told that the library was also still furnished, along with the tale of the viscount's generosity to the cottagers, went there with the girls after dinner, and announced she would read to them.

Amanda and Clarissa stared at her in dumb fury. They had had a terrible day. The thought of new gowns bored them. Having to be polite for a whole day, a thing neither could remember having done before, was tiresome and exhausting. And now she was going to read to them.

But mindful of the viscount's threat, they settled down in the library.

In St. Giles Jean had bought three volumes of one of the latest novels. Although the girls were obviously in need of moral instruction, she was sure they would simply fall asleep if she tried to read a book of sermons. The first thing, Jean decided, was to get them interested in any form of literature, and Jean guiltily admitted to herself she had also bought the books for her own enjoyment.

She started to read. Amanda and Clarissa, slumped side by side on the sofa, listened, at first stifling yawns and then with growing interest. When the headless monk walked down the stairs of the castle in Italy and Lady Felicity swooned in the prince's arms, they sat up. Jean read on while the girls leaned forward, finally hanging on every word.

A footman came in, lit a log fire in the grate, and retreated quietly.

An hour later the door opened and the weary viscount walked in.

He stood for a moment, surveying the scene. Jean Morrison was reading steadily, the light from an oil lamp above her head shining on her magnificent hair. The fire crackled cheerfully, and Mrs. Moody, inspired to artistic talent by the increase in wages, had filled bowls around the room with scarlet and red roses.

Jean saw him and stopped reading. "Go on," the twins cried in unison.

"Tomorrow," Jean promised with a smile. "I did not realize how late it was, my lord. Bed for you, young ladies."

"Stay, Miss Morrison," the viscount said. "Amanda and Clarissa, you will find a lady's maid waiting for you. She is not very well trained, but she will do for the moment. Treat her with courtesy."

Amanda and Clarissa went out and closed the door, and then went slowly up the stairs. "If she's going to read us them adventures, why get rid of her?" Clarissa asked.

"Silly, we've got to do our lessons, ain't we?" Amanda remarked. "We'll soon be able to read them ourselves. No governess is going to tell us what to do. Besides, she is only a governess and she shouldn't be sitting with the master. Get ideas above her station. Think he'll ruin her?"

"Don't think he sees her as a woman and that's a fact," Clarissa commented.

In their bedchamber a burly-looking woman was waiting for them. She silently brushed their hair, got them ready for bed, and tucked them in. Clarissa felt guiltily that it was pleasant to be cared for, and she liked her new clean hair that felt silky to the touch. But she adored Amanda and everything that Amanda said or did must be right.

"Did you have any trouble with them today?" the viscount was asking Jean.

"No, they behaved very well, my lord, and I am convinced they are good at heart. I gather that a great deal of furniture has gone from the castle to the cottagers."

He told her of his day while her green eyes glowed with admiration.

"You are very good."

"I am motivated by my own interest. I have been

41

studying the accounts. Mr. Courtney inherited a fortune to begin with and then made more over the years by gradually raising the rents. In the past few years the power of making people miserable far outweighed the pleasure of money."

"How dreadful! It is no wonder that Amanda and Clarissa have turned out the way they are."

"I think, on the contrary, they were treated with indulgence by their father. That is what ruined them. They were allowed to do and say as they liked and not one servant was allowed to reprimand them. I think they have inherited their father's—if he was their father—love of power to cause misery."

Jean looked at him uneasily. "I feel you are too harsh. I know they behaved disgracefully by pushing me in that tarn, but I cannot help feeling that a horsewhipping was the wrong sort of punishment."

"They were not horsewhipped."

"But the screams of anguish . . . the cries for help."

"They were enduring a bath. Cleanliness is a form of refined torture to their minds. They have been unusually meek and biddable since, but that may be because of my threat to hand them over to the authorities if they stepped out of line again. Nonetheless, you should be on your guard at all times."

"There is the matter of pin money for them," Jean said. "Have you thought of that?"

"Yes, I will give you a sum each quarter for them, and you can give them money when the occasion demands it. I assume they have not had any since their father died."

"And yet their room was full of boxes of chocolates and sugarplums," Jean mused. "I took it upon myself to give all the sweetmeats to the staff. I wonder where they got the money to buy such a quantity?"

"Probably had a great deal left over from whatever allowance their father gave them. Do you plan to diet them—like Byron—on potatoes and vinegar?"

"I am sure with exercise and normal, healthful meals, they will soon be a more pleasing shape."

"I see the piano has been moved down here," he said, looking over his shoulder. "Play something for me, Miss Morrison."

She obediently went to the piano and began to play. When she finally looked around, the viscount was fast asleep.

Jean went over to him and stood for a few moments, looking down. It was odd to think of a man as being beautiful, but the viscount had an extraordinary beauty. His golden hair was tumbled over his brow. She half put out a hand to smooth it back from his brow. His eyes opened, and he stared up at her sleepily.

Jean snatched her hand back and stammered out, "Good night" before fleeing from the room.

Chapter Three

DURING THE TWO WEEKS that followed, Jean Morrison was happier than she had ever been before. The days were cloudless and warm and full of activity. In the mornings she would start teaching her two charges at eight o'clock promptly and continue until noon, when a cold collation would be served in the schoolroom. In the afternoons she would supervise riding lessons for the girls, having learned, to her surprise, that they did not know how to ride.

There were a few nasty little battles in the early days because Amanda and Clarissa blamed their horses for every fall and would have thrashed the poor animals had they not been forcibly restrained by Jean and the grooms. Slowly they mastered the art and came to enjoy it. After the riding lessons, there were fittings for their new gowns and then some piano practice.

Jean looked forward to the highlight of the day, which was dinner, when she could sit across the table from the viscount and listen to his pleasant voice. And after dinner they would retire to the library and Jean would read to them all, the viscount finding it more pleasant to listen to her soft Scottish voice than to sit in solitary state in the dining room with the port decanter.

He did feel at times ludicrously like a settled family man, watching the glow of Jean's bright hair in the lamplight and seeing the now-slimmer twins sitting, holding hands, listening intently to every word. Their reading skills had improved immensely, but, like the viscount, they enjoyed Jean's readings although they could not for the world have admitted such, telling each other that it was as well to see the governess earned her keep.

The viscount was also beginning to bask in a rare feeling of achievement. The ins and outs of agriculture were daily becoming more interesting. He also found himself thinking more of cottagers as people and less as some rare breed of cattle who had to be kept in good coat. A school was going to be built on the estate and also a small church, the nearest church being in St. Giles. He had been surprised to find that Jean Morrison thought it his duty to hold a service on Sunday mornings in the hall of the castle for the servants and tenants, and he had amiably complied although looking forward to the day when the church would be completed and some vicar would take the burden of religious instruction off his hands.

To his surprise, the vicar of St. Anne's in St. Giles refused point-blank to come to the castle and undertake the religious instruction of the girls. He said he was too busy, and even the offer of generous funds for his church would not sway him. The viscount could only assume that the girls' bad reputation had spread into the town.

On one such evening, stretched out in a comfortable chair, he listened to Jean's voice and wondered idly what his friends were doing in London. Now that the castle was being refurbished and most of the dust and gloom swept away, London seemed less of a desirable place.

And then he heard the sound of carriages outside followed by a great knocking at the door.

"Who can be calling so late?" he asked as Jean stopped her reading and looked up in surprise. The twins suddenly looked at each other and exchanged smiles—long, slow, secretive smiles.

Dredwort entered. "Some gentlemen have arrived and an . . . er . . . lady, my lord." He presented the viscount with four cards.

"Show them in," the viscount cried, reading only the first card, that of Lord Charnworth.

His three friends came sailing into the room, propelling Nancy Cruze, his mistress, in front of them. Nancy was in full fig—scarlet gown cut as low as the nipples, glossy brown hair, paint as thick as stage makeup on her pretty little face.

Jean Morrison rose to her feet. "Clarissa and Amanda," she ordered in a cold voice, "come with me."

"But we ain't been introduced yet," Amanda said, her little black eyes dancing with mischief.

"That will not be necessary. Do as you are bid!" And thrusting the girls before her, Jean left the room, her head held high.

"Who was that ladybird?" Mr. Trump asked.

"The governess of distinction," the viscount replied with a rueful look. "But what brings you all here?"

"Your letter," Lord Charnworth said with a laugh.

Nancy wound her white arms around the viscount, but he gently pushed her away and demanded, "What letter?"

"Paul's got it," Mr. Trump said, and Mr. Jolly produced a crumpled letter from his pocket and handed it over.

The viscount read it carefully. "I did not write this," he said. He turned it over and examined the broken seal. "But it's my seal and a fair approximation of my handwriting, too. Not that I am not glad to see you, although you are come at an awkward time. I have so much work to do."

Nancy pouted prettily. "I thought you was pining for me."

"But of course. But not here, not now. You must realize the circumstances. Demme, who wrote that letter?"

He rang the bell and ordered wine and cakes for the party and for bedchambers to be allotted to them, and then asked Dredwort to fetch Miss Morrison.

The butler was gone some time, and when he returned, he said with a wooden face, "Miss Morrison begs your pardon, my lord, and says she would prefer to speak to you in private. She awaits you in the drawing room."

"Things have changed," Mr. Trump drawled. "Getting your orders from a governess?"

"Wait here. I will not be long." The viscount strode out and mounted the stairs to the drawing room. Jean was waiting there for him, a trifle pale, but composed.

"Miss Morrison," he began, "I am deeply grateful to you for the change in Amanda and Clarissa, but it is not your place to summon me."

She looked at him solemnly. "I have no objection

47

to appearing before your friends, but I must do all I can to continue to improve the sadly debased morals of Amanda and Clarissa. Should I stoop to be on familiar terms with what is obviously a female of the demimonde, I should not be setting them a good example."

He gave a harsh laugh. "You may find your little innocents were instrumental in bringing that ladybird here." He thrust the letter at her. "Read this."

She quickly scanned it and then raised puzzled green eyes to his. "I do not understand."

"I did not write it. It is a forgery."

Jean looked at the letter again. "Although the girls are much improved in literacy, they could never have achieved this, and how could they know whom to write to?"

"If you will remember, they asked me for the names of my friends and I mentioned the three downstairs. If they did not write it, then they must have asked someone to do it for them."

"But that would require a degree of planning and villainy surely beyond two young girls. And they have hardly been out of my sight."

"Except when you are asleep."

"Give me the letter and I will tax them with it. But you must understand my position, my lord. While that lady is in the house, I cannot allow either myself or the girls to come near her. I did not think it customary to have such persons in one's family home."

He was suddenly very angry. "Don't dare take that high moral line with me, Miss Morrison."

She gazed at him stubbornly. "Oh, take your

meals in the schoolroom in future," he snapped. "Your long face would put a damper on any party."

Jean stayed where she was for a long time after he had left. She felt she was looking down at pieces of clay strewn about her feet. Her idol had toppled off his pedestal. She was not in love with the viscount, but in the preceding days she had hero-worshipped him. It was not only his good looks that had seduced her aesthetic senses, but his goodness to his tenants. He had said that his openhanded-ness to the cottagers had been self-interest. Estates well run were profitable estates. She had put that down to manly modesty, that he was veiling his goodness. Now she had to believe him. A man of principle would have turned that painted harlot from his doors. As Jean thought of the "painted harlot," tears rolled down her cheeks. She had had an illusion of a home during the past two weeks. Now it was shattered. She hoped for a moment that there would be nowhere for these unwelcome guests to sleep and then remembered that new beds had been delivered only two days before, modern beds without posts or hangings, although canopies of a sort were being made to be fitted over the heads of the bed later.

She carefully dried her eyes and went up to Amanda and Clarissa's bedchamber. They were both sitting upright in the large bed that they shared, looking expectantly toward the door.

Jean held out the letter. "How did you get this written?" she demanded harshly.

Their little black eyes opened to their fullest in innocent surprise. "Us!" Clarissa exclaimed. And then realizing her error said quickly, "What letter?"

"I am sure you know very well what I am speaking about," Jean said, suddenly weary. "But you have achieved your aim. I do have some standards. I am not going to stay under the same roof as that woman. Lord Hunterdon may find you another governess."

Amanda's mind worked quickly. If Miss Morrison went, there would be no more stories from this Scheherazade. But she could not think of anything to say.

"In any case, I am sure you are both very happy to have achieved your aim," Jean said.

She went to her own room and slowly began to pack her trunks. She glanced at herself in the mirror. She was wearing one of her new gowns, thin India muslin ornamented with little green silk leaves. How she had hoped he would notice how well she looked in it only earlier that evening! Should she leave him a letter to say he could keep the new gowns? But she had worked for them, and deserved them because Amanda and Clarissa had damaged some of her old ones. It was highly unlikely she would ever have such pretty clothes again. She worked for a long time, trying not to think of the viscount lying in the arms of "that woman."

When she had finally finished packing, she sat down and wrote the viscount a short letter saying that he would appreciate the fact that she could no longer, under the circumstances, remain in his employ.

In the morning she handed the letter to Dredwort as one of the footmen loaded her trunks into the castle gig. The normally uncommunicative Dredwort begged her to stay, but Jean was adamant.

Dredwort gloomily watched her go.

The viscount had not spent the night in the arms of his mistress, much to her surprise. But he had passed a pleasant evening with his friends, talking gossip and drinking deep.

He awoke the next day and looked in bleary surprise at the clock. Ten in the morning! He was not accustomed to sleeping so late. His head felt heavy and his stomach queasy. He realized ruefully that he had become used to feeling healthy in the mornings. There was still so much to be done and yet he must entertain his friends, and what was to be done with Nancy? His face hardened. Jean Morrison would just have to get used to her presence.

His guests were not awake when he went downstairs. He assumed they would keep London hours and rise about two in the afternoon. He climbed up to the schoolroom to give himself the pleasure of putting his governess firmly in her place, but found it empty.

Feeling strangely flat, he went downstairs and rode out to check the improvements to his estates. He became so absorbed in the repairs to buildings and the crops in fields that he quite forgot about the situation waiting for him at home. When he returned, he found his friends and Nancy eating hearty breakfasts.

"Have you seen Miss Morrison?"

"Your Scotch governess? Neither she nor the little girls have been about," Lord Charnworth said, spearing a kidney. "What have you got planned for us today, hey?"

"In a minute." The viscount strode out and went to the stairs to go up to the schoolroom. Dredwort waylaid him and handed him a letter. "Later," the viscount said.

"It is from Miss Morrison." Dredwort spoke in hushed tones, as if announcing the death of a relative.

The viscount broke the seal and read what Jean had written. "A pox on her," he said savagely. "I'll advertise for another one."

"If I may make so bold, my lord," Dredwort began.

"Oh, make away. This looks like being a filthy day anyway."

"I cannot think that there is any female in the whole of Dorset as highly qualified as Miss Morrison. We have had many governesses here . . . weak, spineless creatures, if I may say so, my lord. To take charge of the Misses Courtney requires razor-sharp wits and a great deal of moral strength. If I may talk man-to-man on this one important occasion . . . ?"

"Get on with it."

"From what I have heard of London, my lord, there are more lightskirts than there are decent women. A good governess is irreplaceable, a Cyprian is not."

The viscount flushed angrily. "How dare you, Dredwort. Miss Cruze is a respectable lady."

"Your lordship may not have remarked the dress Miss Cruze is wearing at the moment," the butler went on. "It is of very fine India muslin, and Miss Cruze is not wearing a stitch under it. The footmen are impressionable lads, and I have had to confine them belowstairs and serve the company myself. I naturally gained the wrong impression of the lady."

The viscount cursed Nancy under his breath. "I

will speak to you later, Dredwort. Where are the girls?"

"They are in the schoolroom, my lord."

"Here he comes!" Amanda said. She and Clarissa quickly scrubbed their eyes with raw onion. The viscount crashed open the door and surveyed the apparently weeping pair. "I do not know how you did it or who you got to write that scurrilous letter," he raged. "Forgery is a crime, d'you here? Damn the pair of you."

"We never wrote that l-letter," Amanda sobbed. "It's not fair to blame us. It's not our fault that you l-like that sort of woman."

"I am locking you in here," the viscount said grimly, "until I get to the bottom of this. I am sure none of the servants would have written that forgery. You got someone, probably some villain in St. Giles who pens letters for the illiterate."

He went out and locked the door. The twins eyed each other in consternation. "He will get to Gully, and if Gully is in his cups, he will confess all," Amanda said. "We'd best pay him off. And our money is running low."

"But we know how to earn more," Clarissa pointed out.

Amanda prized a floorboard up in the corner of the schoolroom and took a bag of gold and another key to the schoolroom door. The twins let themselves quietly out of the schoolroom and then scurried along to the landing, where they moved a large cabinet away from the wall to reveal a secret door. They opened it and then pulled the cabinet back across it before hurrying down the dark stairs. The stairs led down and then along a damp tunnel that came out among the jumble of huge rocks on the beach. Then they set off for St. Giles at a run to find Gully, pay him the money, and send him away.

The viscount took Nancy and his friends around the estate that afternoon, after Nancy had been ordered to change her gown. But Nancy's appearance, which would not have raised many eyebrows in London, where the ladies of the ton were apt to look like prostitutes, caused dismay among his cottagers and tenant farmers. The viscount could not help noticing that the man of the house shooed his women and children out of sight as soon as he set eyes on Nancy and entertained the viscount and his friends himself. And Nancy, resentful and bored, interlarded her conversation with broad swear words, demanded wine, and became increasingly drunk and noisy. Jean Morrison's sorrowful face rose before the viscount's eyes. He realized at last that he had actually enjoyed being a savior and hero to these people. Because of Nancy he was losing status, and as he watched Nancy reeling about and shouting and singing, he began to see why. There was no way he could impose the likes of this rowdy mistress on the gentle and respectable people of the countryside. He also saw the beginnings of fear and wariness in their eyes.

Mr. Peterman, the agent, who was accompanying him, explained the reason when the viscount demanded angrily what he had done to make everyone afraid of him.

"Your servants thought very highly of the Scottish governess, my lord. Gossip travels quickly in the country and the news is that you let her go rather than get rid of your . . . er . . . lady companion. They do not understand London ways and believe your behavior shows a dangerous fickleness and that you could suddenly turn on them. Most have endured terrible times of hardship and they cannot quite believe their present luck."

"What's up, Beau?" Mr. Jolly asked.

"Demme, it's Nancy." Nancy was in her bedchamber, and the viscount and his friends were sitting in the library, drinking burgundy.

"Thought you'd be delighted," Mr. Trump said.

The viscount sighed heavily. "It's like this. I wouldn't have had Nancy at my house in Town. The servants wouldn't have stood for it. So can you imagine what effect she is having here! Besides, I am responsible for those two brats. If the lawyers get wind of this, then Toad Basil may inherit all. The thought, I admit, is tempting. But I cannot go back to my old life and leave things unfinished here."

Lord Charnworth looked at him sorrowfully. "The fact is, Beau, you've changed."

"How so?"

"Used to be up to every rig and row in Town. Now you've got the cares of the world on your shoulders. There's no *fun* in you anymore. Say goodbye to this place and return with us."

The viscount gave a rueful smile. "In truth, if I left my tenants and farmers to Basil, I would never sleep easy. I am sorry, but I must ask you to leave and take Nancy with you."

"All that way back to London!" Lord Charnworth looked at him in horror. "It's miles and miles and miles. Besides, we've only just arrived here. Think of the noise Nancy will make."

"I'll deal with Nancy. You must see that I did

not write that letter. Of course I will be glad to entertain you anytime, but not with Nancy."

"You'll lose her," Mr. Trump warned. "Lord Tenbar has been trying to get her away from you."

"Then let him. See to your packing and I'll get rid of Nancy."

The viscount went up to Nancy's bedchamber after having written out a generous draft on his bank. Nancy was lying asleep on top of the bedcovers. He studied her for a few moments, wondering why he had ever become involved with her. But how dainty and pretty she had looked on the other side of the footlights. All the men were mad about her, and he had set out to secure her, driven by the spirit of competition. Courtesans such as Harriet Wilson, for example, dubbed the Queen of Tarts, were always in demand because they were in fashion rather than because their charms were superior to those of any other member of the demimonde.

He shook her gently awake. Her eyes opened and she slowly smiled up at him and held up her arms. What, he thought irrationally, would Jean Morrison look like in bed, holding up her arms to her lover? He shook his head angrily.

"Nancy, you must leave. I am sorry, but my friends should not have brought you."

She sat up and scowled at him. "You've turned pompous and respectable, Beau."

"Perhaps. But perhaps this will ease our parting."

She opened her mouth to start to create a scene, but then her eyes fell on the bank draft he was holding out to her and her eyes widened. It was a magnificent sum. Her hands like little claws, closed tightly around it. Nancy, unlike other members of the fashionable impure, was thrifty with money, squirreling away the bulk of it. Her aim was to amass enough and then to retire to some provincial city and take on the character of a lady.

"Do you not want to see me again?" she finally asked.

"No, Nancy, I will be too much occupied here."

"Lord Tenbar is keen for my favors."

"Let him have them, if that is your pleasure."

"That governess has changed you," Nancy said waspishly after she had carefully stowed the bank draft away in her jewel box. She sighed. "Men always fall for that sort of thing."

"What sort of thing, Nancy?"

"The morals of a puritan and a passionate face. Leave me, Beau, before you make that speech about wanting me to leave as soon as possible."

Jean Morrison sat sewing. Her aunt was taking an afternoon nap, but she had left her plenty of sewing and darning to keep her occupied. Mrs. Delmar-Richardson had graciously condescended to forgive her niece, for she had now an unpaid companion for life. Jean read and played the piano so well. Like most women who were incapable of making friends, Mrs. Delmar-Richardson could ignore that fact so long as she had a companion in her power. Various companions had come and gone, finding the harsh regime and the fact that no free time was allowed too much for them.

Thinking her life was over, Jean stitched away diligently and tried not to cry. If only those last two weeks at the castle, before his friends had arrived, had not been so happy and pleasant. And Nancy! How could he?

57

That such things went on, she knew very well. Her aunt in Edinburgh, a stern Calvinist, enjoyed nothing more than talking salaciously about the affairs of the aristocracy over the teacups with her friends. If she had not known Lord Hunterdon and someone had told Jean that he kept an opera dancer, she would not have been shocked in the least, particularly as the viscount was unmarried. She had been unrealistic, Jean told herself sternly. She had wanted the viscount to remain forever on his pedestal, golden and smiling, to be looked up to and admired. She could not have him and therefore no one else should. And yet, whatever her reasons, she could not have remained as governess to two young and impressionable girls with that Cyprian in the same house. She had done what was right and the fact that she gained no pleasure from her actions was just too bad. But she had hoped he would call, even to berate her. During her first few miserable days with her aunt she had comforted herself with visions of what he would say and what she would reply.

Now she felt he would not come. Why should he? All he had to do was to find another governess. Jean was wearing her gray dress, which she was beginning to hate, her aunt having taken one horrified look at her new gowns and pronounced them unsuitable.

No, he would not come, and she, Jean Morrison, would be left to rot here under the thumb of the domestic tyrant that was her aunt.

The twins were in a fury. The days since Jean had left were long and boring and unstructured. They had assumed that as soon as Jean had left, the viscount would get her back. They crept down to the library one night and found the draft of a new advertisement for a governess of distinction.

Amanda missed the readings and Clarissa missed the rides, for the head groom said he would not allow them to take any horses out of the stables unless they were supervised by a governess. Normally they would have then taken out their spite on someone like their lady's maid, Betty, but Betty was such a powerful woman and the viscount had told the servants that they were to report any disobedience on the part of the twins to him, so they could not relieve their feelings that way.

"I think," Amanda said one morning after a restless night of thought, "that we should appeal to his sense of duty."

"What?" Clarissa demanded.

"Well, why doesn't he go back to London instead of riding about seeing that a lot o' peasants are comfortable? Duty, that's what it is. He's got a duty to us although we ain't pointed that out."

"All sounds a bit high and windy to me," Clarissa commented. "Good thing Gully got clear. Hunterdon rode to St. Giles the day after and found out about him, but Gully was far away by then, thank God! Where is our lord and master at this moment?"

Amanda leaned out of the window. "Just come back. It's raining like the devil and he's all wet and muddy. Let's catch him before he goes off again."

They scampered down the stairs. The viscount was just drawing off his gloves. He saw the twins and scowled. "Now what?" he demanded.

"It is very serious," Amanda said, putting her

59

hands behind her back and standing before him like a model schoolgirl.

"What is?"

"Your lack of care for us. We understand that under the terms of our father's will you were to care for us and find us husbands."

"So? You're too young at the moment."

"But how are we going to get any if we're not schooled," Amanda wailed, exasperated. "It's your *duty* to see to our welfare."

What an unlovely pair they are, he thought. "I am doing my duty. I am sending a new advertisement for a governess out today."

"Why go to that trouble?" Amanda demanded. "Get Miss Morrison back."

"How can I get Miss Morrison back? She is probably halfway to Scotland."

"No, she's not," Amanda said triumphantly. "She's at her aunt's in Gunshott."

"And how do you know that?"

"We asked about," Amanda said vaguely. "So she's there."

"May I remind you that Miss Morrison left my employ of her own free will?"

"Miss Morrison left because you brought your light o' love into your own home," Amanda said. "She has a strong sense of duty, you see. *She* cared for us."

He stood for a moment, thinking. It certainly would make life easier if he persuaded Jean Morrison to come back. The house had seemed . . . temporary . . . without her, as if it had lost something. The servants missed her, he knew that, and it was odd that servants would have such regard for a governess, that usually despised class.

"I will write to her."

"No," Amanda said stubbornly, "that won't do. Her aunt may open the letter and she'd never get to hear of it."

"If I go in person, I may never get to see her," he pointed out. "All her aunt has to do is to show me the door."

"Mrs. Delmar-Richardson sleeps in the afternoons between two and four," Amanda said.

"You appear to be remarkably well informed."

The twins stood staring up at him.

"Oh, very well, I will ride over this afternoon. Go away now and do something or other."

Hand in hand the twins mounted the stairs. Amanda stopped on the first landing and turned around. "She took *The Perils of Lady Devere* with her before she'd finished it. Get her to bring it back."

"Don't give me orders," the viscount snapped, but the twins had continued their upward climb.

Jean was very tired. As usual, her aunt had risen at six in the morning and then had gone for a walk, accompanied, of course, by Jean, who had to walk slightly behind her and carry her fan and shawl. Then over breakfast Jean read from Mr. Porteous's sermons. After that she had to check the household accounts and go out to the village and question any shopkeepers whom her aunt felt might be over-charging, which was usually every shopkeeper in the village. Back again to watch her aunt take a "light" luncheon. Jean was not allowed any, breakfast and dinner being considered sufficient for her. During luncheon she read the newspapers to her aunt and played the piano to her after the remains of the meal had been cleared away.

Promptly at two o'clock Mrs. Delmar-Richardson would retire to bed, after having looked out a quantity of sewing for Jean.

The sun was shining outside, the weather having cleared after the morning's rain, but Jean knew she dared not leave her sewing and go out. Her aunt checked every stitch to make sure she had not been slacking.

Jean sighed heavily. This was to be her life from now on. God had decreed it thus. Nothing would ever happen now to change the weary boredom of her days.

The door opened and a maid said, "Lord Hunterdon to see you, miss," and Jean stabbed the needle into her finger in surprise.

The maid did not wait to see if Jean was prepared to see Lord Hunterdon, for poor relations did not have any social standing.

Jean put aside her sewing and stood up as the viscount walked into the room.

She had comforted herself by thinking of him as some debased satyr, and it was upsetting to see him there, golden and elegant, starched cravat, impeccable morning coat, shining boots, and emanating unruffled calm.

He bowed slightly. He began without preamble. "I am come to offer you the post of governess again."

Jean's heart leapt up and then sank when she thought of Nancy.

He studied her downcast face and said impatiently, "My friends have left and, yes, Nancy as well. But although I will not invite any of my . . .

er . . . pleasures to my home again, I do not wish any more of your moral strictures."

"Have you cast her off?" Jean's green eyes looked up at him seriously.

"Yes, if you must know, I have, but that is none of your affair."

"My lord, what will she do now?"

"Miss Morrison! Oh, very well. If you must know . . . She plans to accept the protection of Lord Tenbar."

Jean sighed. "Poor thing. And when Lord Tenbar is tired of her, she will pass to some other gentleman until no one wants her and she is left destitute."

"You have been reading too many novels. I did not seduce Nancy Cruze. She was a well-established member of the demimonde when I took her on and she knew exactly what she was doing. Unlike her kind, she does not indulge in drink and saves as much as she can. By the time she retires from her profession, she will be a wealthy woman. She will reappear in York or some such place under a new name and set up house as a widow and be a pillar of the community. Now, does that put your mind at rest? For I am heartily sick of the Misses Courtneys' complaints about your absence."

"They miss me?" Jean exclaimed. "Why?"

"I cannot begin to imagine. I have much to do. Are you coming or are you not?"

Jean hesitated. Her aunt would never have her back now. Once the twins were safely launched on their Season, her job would be over and she would need to find another and move from household to household until she grew too old and then, unlike Nancy, she would find herself hard put to manage.

But better to live for a few years in comfort and to have something to remember than spend her days in this genteel drudgery.

"I will pack my bags, my lord," she said. "I am not going to wake my aunt, for there would be an awkward scene."

He nodded. "I will wait for you outside."

Jean ran to her room and packed feverishly, terrified her aunt would wake and call for her. Two maids helped her down the stairs with her baggage and said, yes, they would tell the mistress she had gone.

Her luggage was strapped on the back and Jean climbed into the open carriage and sat beside the viscount, who said, "I am going to call on Farmer Tulley on our way back. I ordered phosphates for his fields and want to make sure they have been delivered."

Jean sat beside him, suddenly very happy. As they mounted a rise, she could see the curtains of rain moving out to sea, and, inclined to be fanciful in her happiness, imagined the rain curtains as being the curtains of a theater, opening on a whole new act in her life.

They drove up to Tulley's farm. "Wait here," the viscount ordered curtly. "Certainly," Jean Morrison replied primly, like any correct governess knowing her place. He tethered the horses and walked into the farmhouse. Jean sat for a few moments in the carriage and then climbed down and walked a little way away, for he had stopped the carriage in the yard next to the dung heap.

She leaned on the fence at the far end of the yard and looked out over the nearest field, which was a carpet of tiny blue flax flowers interspersed with blazing scarlet poppies. It seemed an outrageous burst of color in the normal green and brown of an English farm landscape. Bees hummed among the flowers and a lark sang overhead. Clouds of tiny blue butterflies as blue as the flax flowers fluttered erratically on the lightest of summer breezes. The sun was warm. She untied the ribbons of her bonnet and took it off, enjoying the heat of the sun on her bare head.

She heard a quick footstep behind her and turned. A stout, red-faced woman was hurrying toward her. "I am Mrs. Tulley," she said, "and you be Miss Morrison, the governess. I said to his lordship that you should step indoors and try some of my lemonade, for it's a mortal hot and dusty day."

"You are very kind," Jean said with a smile.

They walked back together to the farmhouse. "You must tell me all about your life," Jean said. "I know very little of farming."

"Don't they have farms in your part of the country, miss?"

"Yes, but not like this, not in the Highlands. It is all heathland and sheep. Very few crops. That is, in the far north, of course."

Mrs. Tulley led the way into the stone-flagged farm kitchen where the viscount sat at his ease at the scrubbed table. "Here's Miss Morrison," Mrs. Tulley said. "I gather she is going back to the castle, my lord."

He raised his eyebrows superciliously. "Gossiping, Miss Morrison?"

"Her hasn't said a word." The farmer's wife poured Jean a glass of lemonade. "Stands to reason, that's all. We all heard she had left and now she's back."

Mrs. Tulley began to tell Jean of the new piano-forte they had bought and Jean said she would like to see it after she had finished her lemonade. The viscount, as Mr. Tulley was telling him about the delivery of the phosphates, glanced at Jean. What was it Nancy had said? Something about puritanism and passion? Her mouth was certainly beautifully shaped. Could this correct governess ever be passionate? Jean caught his cool blue speculative look and suddenly blushed.

It struck her at that moment that he wasn't a god, nor a fallen idol either, but a man: a sensual, attractive, highly desirable man.

She rose quickly to her feet and urged Mrs. Tulley to show her the piano. She followed her from the room with a feeling of relief. She must never think of her employer like that again.

It was not . . . correct.

Chapter Four

For a while Jean found the days pleasant. The girls treated her with as much courtesy as she could expect, considering their characters. But a change came about when Jean finally ran through the small stock of novels available in St. Giles. The viscount sent an order to a London bookseller for a selection of the latest works and so Jean decided to fill in the intervening time by improving the girls' moral tone with readings from the Bible.

The viscount did not particularly notice the change because he simply liked to relax in the evenings and listen to Jean's soft Scottish voice, no matter what she read, but the twins were restless and bored and resentful. Jean began to wonder if they were ill, for they began to appear in the schoolroom in the mornings heavy-eyed and listless. They were also becoming unhealthily fat again. She doubted if they would ever possess elegant figures even when they lost their puppy fat, but by carefully monitoring what they ate, she had experienced the pleasure of noticing that their skin was clear and that they were less lumpy in shape than when she had first taken up her post. But now they were spotty, their hair was dull, and their new gowns were having to be let out.

She sent for a physician, who prescribed Dr. James's powders after diagnosing a temporary disorder of the spleen. The next afternoon Amanda and Clarissa, who had been barely attending to their studies in the morning, begged leave to be allowed to take a nap. Left to her own devices, Jean went out for a walk. In the distance she saw the tall figure of the viscount, supervising the work of a team of gardeners and laborers who were landscaping the gardens. She walked a little nearer, hoping the viscount would call to her and perhaps discuss his plans for the gardens with her, but he was too absorbed in his work and so she turned away and walked around the back of the house and down through what used to be terraced gardens and were now a riot of weeds, to the beach.

The day was still and overcast. Large glassy waves curved onto the beach and fanned out slowly over the sands. The weather was close and humid and there did not seem to be a breath of air. Jean felt sad and listless. On such a day when she had time on her hands, she became acutely aware of her situation, that she was only a governess, a paid servant. All she had to comfort her was a wicked little dream at the back of her mind that her aunt in Edinburgh, who was extremely rich, would die and leave her all her money so that she, Jean Morrison, would become a lady of independent means, a lady with a dowry, a marriageable lady.

She walked beyond the point on the beach where she had previously veered off to follow the twins to the tarn. There were large jagged rocks at the end with only a strip of beach in front of them. The tide was out, so it would not normally be possible to walk past this outcrop. A sea gull screamed harshly, and suddenly, as the shadow of the rocks fell over her and to her right, another sea gull seemed to answer. She looked up and about, but could see no birds in the still, gray landscape where the only moving thing was the slow rise and fall of the ocean. She walked around the outcrop and found a stretch of cliffs and a series of caves. Looking nervously back, for she did not want to be cut off by the sea should the tide come in, she went into the first of the caves to explore. It was large and empty with a smooth, sandy floor. Festoons of green and wetly glittering seaweed hung down from the rocky walls. A splash of color near the cave entrance caught her eye, and she stooped down to examine it. There were several sweetmeat wrappings fluttering to and fro in the breeze that had suddenly risen outside. Out of the damp sand protruded the edge of a box. Jean dug with her fingers until she had pulled a wet and soggy cardboard box lid from the sand. She sat back on her heels and looked thoughtfully on her find. It looked as if someone had eaten the chocolates or sweetmeats and then buried the evidence, but the tide had washed the sand away and some of the exposed wrappings that were now fluttering and scurrying like mice over the cave floor had been dried after the tide had receded. It might be the twins. And yet, if they were not under her supervision, Betty, the maid, kept a close eye on them. But it would explain their increased weight and spotty faces if they had been creeping out from the castle to buy sweetmeats. She frowned down at the box and wrappers. She picked up one of the wrappers. It had a few slight traces of chocolate in the wrinkles of the twisted paper. Only the most expensive of confectionery was boxed, and the confection-

69

ers in St. Giles did not sell such delicacies, only things such as toffees or fudge, licorice laces and candied nuts. Only a small proportion of the population of the British Isles had tasted chocolate sweets, although more were familiar with the breakfast drink. When an English general had escaped from the Jacobites in Scotland and his carriage seized, it was found to contain boxes of little rolls of chocolate. But the Highlanders thought it must be medicine and so sold the loot, claiming it to be a wonderful salve for wounds. So if the Courtney girls had indeed been eating such chocolate, where did it come from and *when* did they eat it?

At night, thought Jean suddenly. That explains the tiredness and heavy eyes. They would deny it only if she accused them of it. She must return to the castle and take a nap herself, and so be prepared to spend the night watching the door of their bedchamber.

The sound of waves outside the cave sounded closer. She hurried out.

The tide had turned, and long, smooth waves were already sweeping up to the base of the outcrop, driven by a stiffening breeze. She removed her shoes and stockings, carried her bonnet over her arm by the ribbons, kilted up her skirts, and ran.

When she gained the smooth crescent of beach below the castle, she slowed her steps and finally stopped, looking with pleasure out to sea. The sky above was clearing rapidly to a deep intense blue, and the breeze was whipping and chopping at the surface of the water, making it dance with a myriad of lights.

She sat down in the sand and stretched her wet feet out to dry.

The library windows overlooked the beach. The viscount stood looking down at the small figure far below on the beach which he knew was Jean Morrison by the splash of fiery red that was her hair.

He felt hot and sticky and gritty, for he had helped in some of the work. He had half a mind to go and join her, but at that moment Dredwort entered and announced he had callers and with a little sigh the viscount said he would change and then join them in the Green Saloon, which was next to the library and had just been painted and refurbished.

Jean, returning slowly from the beach a half hour later and planning to have that nap, was met by a footman who told her that Lord Hunterdon had callers and that she and the Misses Courtney were to present themselves in the Green Saloon.

She went quickly up to the twins' bedchamber. They were having their hair braided by Betty and had already been changed into clean gowns. Jean went to her own room and washed and changed into one of her new gowns, brushed and arranged her curly red hair in one of the new Roman styles, and then, satisfied with her appearance, went to collect the twins.

A maid had told Jean that the callers were Lord and Lady Pemberton who had estates on the other side of St. Giles. Jean, entering the Green Saloon with the girls in front of her, realized at last her new position in the social pecking order. Her gown of India muslin, high-waisted, white with little gold corn ears embroidered all over it, she suddenly knew was too fashionable for a governess, as Lady Pemberton raised her quizzing glass and gave Jean a long, slow stare of disapproval. While the twins

71

were introduced, Jean went quietly to a chair in the corner by the window and sat down demurely although her heart was racing. For Lady Pemberton had brought her daughters with her, pretty daughters, *marriageable* daughters. One, the elder, Letitia, aged nineteen, had dark brown glossy curls, a little pouting mouth, and a curvaceous figure. Her sister, Ann, aged eighteen, had chestnut hair, a thinner figure, and an air of glacial superiority. Lady Pemberton was a small, fussy woman, overdressed, overjeweled, overberibboned. Lord Pemberton was tall and thin and angular with a long, sad face and weak, watery gray eyes.

Letitia was flirting with the viscount, telling him that the whole county was dying to meet him, while sister Ann adopted an Attitude, one arm outstretched and the other to her brow. Jean wondered acidly what it was supposed to represent.

"Of course, we were not on calling terms with Mr. Courtney," Lady Pemberton said, "and when he married a *servant*, well, enough said on that subject. We are gratified to have such an elegant member of the ton among us, Lord Hunterdon, and we are called to ask you to dine with us next week. A turtle dinner."

"Good," Amanda said, finding her voice. "We like turtle."

Lady Pemberton favored her with a wintry smile. "You are still too young, my child, to be *out*. Perhaps another time."

"Ain't you asking us?" Clarissa demanded.

"You really must get that governess of yours to correct your grammar." Lady Pemberton gave a brittle laugh. "Now, Lord Hunterdon, I am sure you will favor us with your presence. We have a further

72

incentive. We have a house guest. None other than your cousin, Mr. Devenham."

"Mr. Devenham is really quite charming," Letitia murmured, fluttering her eyelashes at the viscount while Ann changed to another Attitude, supporting her chin on the backs of her hands and staring nobly into space.

"How very kind of you to ask me," the viscount said, "but could I possibly visit you at some later date? You will see from the upheaval in the grounds and in the house that I am in the midst of improvements."

"Come, come, Hunterdon," Lord Pemberton said. "We're talking about *dinner*. Can't carry on with work in the evening."

"Oh, but I do," the viscount said ruefully. "I work from dawn to dusk, I assure you. But I shall call on you quite soon."

Lady Pemberton gave him a baffled look and then her eyes swung around to where Jean was sitting. Was that overfashionably dressed governess with the ridiculous color hair the reason for the viscount's reluctance to accept invitations? It was well known he had already invited a Cyprian to his home, although he had quickly got rid of her.

"Miss . . . whatever your name is," Lady Pemberton commanded, "come here. I wish to ask you a few questions."

Jean obediently rose and crossed the room to stand in front of Lady Pemberton, who demanded, "What are your qualifications?"

The viscount's voice was suddenly cold. "Are you intent on employing my governess?" he asked.

"Of course not," Lady Pemberton said. "But I feel you gentlemen are not quite up to the mark when it comes to the employment of female servants. For example, her dress is quite unsuitable, and with hair that color she should be made to wear a cap."

"As I said before, I have much to do," the viscount said, "and must beg you to excuse me. Miss Morrison, take the Misses Courtney to the schoolroom, if you please."

Jean was conscious of the glacial atmosphere as she shepherded the twins from the room.

"Old cat," Amanda said loudly and viciously while she was still within hearing range of the guests.

"Silence!" Jean ordered. "I will talk to both of you upstairs."

In the schoolroom she told them to take their places and then began. "I will tell you this privately—Lady Pemberton is a rude and overbearing woman. You will meet many such when you go into society, but you must learn how to deal with them. Lady Pemberton has two marriageable daughters and Lord Hunterdon must be regarded as a great catch. Had she been a clever woman, she would have included both of you in the invitation. On the other hand, there is no reason why she should, for you have both not yet been presented. You should not have made any comment at all, Amanda, but simply waited in silence. Had you not, then I have no doubt that Lord Hunterdon would have assumed you were both included in the invitation and he would have taken you along. If you are displeased with someone, polite silence can be an effective weapon. Now, there will be more callers and more parents, not just interested in Lord Hunterdon, but in the pair of you, perhaps with a view to securing you for their sons when you come of age. I have no doubt Lord Hunterdon has arranged or will arrange generous dowries for both of you. So in the future, when in doubt as to what to say, sit modestly quiet."

Two pairs of small black eyes surveyed her. "What would you ha' done," Clarissa asked, "if Hunterdon hadn't stepped in to shut her up?"

"As a governess and paid servant, I would have had to endure any questioning."

"And what was that Ann creature about?" Amanda asked. "Grimacing and staring."

"She was adopting Attitudes," Jean said, repressing a smile.

"What's an Attitude?"

"Well, it is a bit of play-acting designed to show some lady's charms to the best advantage. For example, if a lady were on a balcony, she could grasp the edge and throw her head back. That would be Juliet after the departure of Romeo. This Attitude would be chosen if the lady had a long and white neck which she wished to show to advantage. It also shows the . . . er . . . shoulders in a flattering light."

"Load o' rubbish," Amanda grumbled.

"It can be impressive if done with grace, and grace of movement is what you both lack. Firstly, if you do not sit up straight, I shall need to strap both of you into backboards. A lady's back should never touch the back of the seat. We will start by walking around the room with books on our head. Remember, when walking, you should never look at your feet, nor should you look behind you when you sit down. A footman will always be there to place the chair correctly for you."

While the twins began to pace up and down, occasionally tripping over their feet and giggling and colliding with each other, Jean thought of that visit. Lady Pemberton had been correct about one thing. She, Jean, was not wearing suitable dress for a governess.

So at dinner that evening she changed into her old gray gown. The viscount was usually silent during dinner, but he followed them through to the library afterward and Jean saw, with delight, that a new consignment of novels had arrived by the carrier.

Jean picked up the top book. It was *Pride and Prejudice* by Jane Austen, a slim book, not like the other huge volumes of romance.

She settled down comfortably under the lamp and began to read. For once the viscount found himself listening to the words and becoming as engrossed in the tale as the rest.

She read on while the light faded outside and a scent of roses crept in through the open windows. At last she reluctantly closed the book, saying she would continue on the morrow, but sympathizing for once with the girls' cries for more.

"A moment," the viscount said as she was leaving the room. "Go ahead, Amanda and Clarissa. Miss Morrison will be with you shortly."

Jean waited in some trepidation, wondering whether Lady Pemberton had encouraged him to get rid of her.

"I could not help noticing you were wearing one of your old gowns," he said.

"Lady Pemberton was effective in reminding me of the unsuitability of my dress," Jean said, but with a little spurt of gladness that he had actually had enough interest to notice what she was wearing.

"But you work for me, not Lady Pemberton, and there is no reason for you to be badly gowned. I think in the future it would be better to describe you as the girls' companion. That will perhaps protect you from further impertinence."

"Thank you, my lord."

He looked up at her curiously as she stood before him. "You have a hard job," he said. "Amanda and Clarissa are remarkably unlovable."

"Oh, no, my lord. All they lack is grace and manners."

"As you will. But if I were you, I would remember at all times that they tried to kill you."

"A girlish prank!"

"I prefer still to think of it as a murderous attempt. Take care, Miss Morrison."

Jean went slowly up the stairs. Poor Amanda and Clarissa, poor orphans, she thought. They have only me to love them, and I must do my best.

She sat down at the writing desk in her room and wrote a courteous letter to her aunt in Edinburgh, happy now to be able to describe her position as that of companion rather than governess. Her duty done, she went quietly to the twins' bedchamber. Both were lying with their eyes closed, their unbraided hair tumbled over the pillows.

Poor things, thought Jean again, and she gently stooped over each girl and kissed her forehead.

Then she went outside and sat down on a chair a little way along the passage. If they woke up and tried to go out, she would catch them.

Inside the bedchamber Amanda nudged Clarissa. "Are you awake?"

" 'Course I'm awake," Clarissa grumbled. "Did she slobber over you as well?"

"Yes. Nearly made me puke. Well, let's get dressed. We've got work to do."

As soon as they were dressed and ready, Amanda cautiously opened the door and then drew back sharply. "What's amiss?" Clarissa demanded.

"*She's* sitting out there—on guard."

"What! The Scotch bitch?"

"The same."

"Damn! How did the bloody whore find out we went out at night, and why didn't she say anything?"

"Trying to trap us."

"Wait a bit," Clarissa said, "if she knew what we really were up to, there would be hell to pay. She wouldn't keep a hanging matter to herself, now, would she?"

Amanda scowled horribly in concentration. "Betty said she was down on the beach this afternoon. Did we bury that chocolate box or didn't we?"

"Did, right in the cave."

"I know," Amanda said, her face clearing. "She's a bit soppy, ain't she? We walk along and ask her sweetly what she's a-doin' of. Don't she trust us and so forth."

Jean was nearly asleep when she heard them approach. "Now, girls, what is this?" she demanded.

"I couldn't sleep, miss," Amanda said seriously, "and I planned to go down to the kitchens for some bread and butter. I put my head around the door and there you was. So I woke Clarissa and we came to find out."

Jean looked at their serious faces, lit from underneath by the flame of the candle on the floor beside her chair. How odd, thought Jean inconsequently, that faces lit by candlelight from underneath always look sinister. She decided to tell the truth. "I assumed," she said finally, "that the boxes of sweetmeats I found in your room were left over from a supply ordered for you by your father, for St. Giles does not sell anything so expensive. Was it you who left the empty box in the cave?"

"Yes," Amanda said. "But we buried it."

"The tide had uncovered it. But how did you get it and when did you go to the cave?"

"There was a box in our room you missed," Amanda said. "We went to the cave the morning of the day you were due to return."

Surely the tides would have disintegrated the box by now, thought Jean. But she did so want to believe them.

"You must not eat chocolates again," she said gently. "Your skin is lovely when you do not and your figures were becoming quite distinguished. Now we will all go to bed and say no more about it."

Amanda leaned down and kissed Jean on the cheek. "Thank you for believing us," she said. And then Clarissa, too, kissed Jean.

Jean blinked back tears, and she stood up and gave them both a hug. "Now, off to bed with you," she said. She returned to her own room and for a while could not sleep because she was so elated, so happy, over those tender little signs of growing trust and affection.

Next morning the viscount stood in the hall, looking down in amusement at Jean as she proudly told him of how the twins had actually kissed her. "And they are not normally given to demonstrations of affection," she said.

"No," he agreed with a smile. "So that should put you on your guard. And they were simply on their way to the kitchens. In their night rail?"

"They were fully dressed, but it is a long way to the kitchens."

"Before you came, Amanda and Clarissa used to wander around the house in their undress until the afternoon. It seems to me that they have more chocolates hidden outside the castle and planned to go out. They are quite cunning. They calculated you would be disarmed by a show of affection, and so you were. Poor Miss Morrison. So eager for kisses?"

Jean colored angrily. "I was merely pleased to think I was doing my job well, my lord. Now I must return to the schoolroom."

He watched her mount the stairs and wondered ruefully what had prompted him to make a flirtatious remark to a governess.

The twins, noticing Jean's steely eyes and the way she went briskly about the morning's lessons, came to the uneasy conclusion that they might not have fooled her at all.

And that night, when they cautiously opened the door of their room and saw her sitting on guard as she had done the night before, became convinced of it.

"Now what are we to do?" Clarissa asked. "I'm getting mortal sick o' this governess. How do we frighten her away? Can't ill treat her or *he'll* step in."

Amanda sat and scowled as she always did when she thought hard. At last she said, "Do you 'member you asked her if she believed in ghosts? And she look half ashamed but said she did? And we've got a ghost."

"Oh, you mean the gray lady the servants talk about. But no one's ever seen her."

"They're going to now," Amanda said with a grin. "Here's my plan. . . ."

In order to continue the slimming process, Jean took the twins out walking the following afternoon. Amanda began to talk about the ghost of the gray lady.

"And where does she walk?" Jean asked.

"The long gallery, above the hall," Clarissa said.

"And what is the story of the gray lady?"

"Well," Amanda said eagerly, "it was when Trelawney Castle really was a castle, in the last century. Her name was Mary Courtney and she was a great heiress. She fell in love with one of the grooms and tried to run off with him. But one of his friends betrayed them to Mr. Jasper Courtney, who was the master then. She was sent home while they took that there groom up to the cliffs and threw him over into the sea. She went mad after that and did nothing else but pace up and down the gallery."

"But how could she pace up and down the gallery if it wasn't this house but the old castle?" Jean asked sharply.

"The hall and gallery are to the same plan as the great hall and gallery in the old castle," Amanda said quickly, and Clarissa threw her sister a look of admiration.

"These old stories are fascinating," Jean said, "but they are only stories. I mean, has anyone seen her?"

"I have," Amanda said in a low voice.

Jean tried to keep her voice light, although she experienced a superstitious Highland shiver of dread. "And what did she look like? Did she give you good eee?"

"I couldn't see her face," Amanda said, she and Clarissa having already decided on the costume. "She's veiled all in gray and she do moan dreadful."

"She does moan dreadfully," Jean corrected her automatically. She gave another little shiver. Gusts of wind were blowing storm clouds in from the sea.

That evening she said good night to the girls, but when she returned to her room to find a book to keep her awake while she guarded the corridor, the twins slipped out and hastened to the long gallery.

Amanda quickly took out her disguise from the bottom drawer of a china cabinet. The sky outside had cleared, and great shafts of moonlight were striking down through the windows and onto the long gallery. The twins had discovered piles of gray gauze in a trunk in the attics, an old-fashioned gown and high-heeled shoes to increase Amanda's height.

"Now what?" Clarissa demanded, stifling a nervous giggle.

"As planned. You know where to hide and keep the door open for me. Now I got to moan, loud enough so as to bring her but not loud enough so as to wake anyone else. Here goes!"

Jean was reading a romance. It was full of ghosts and horrors. And then she realized that the faint ghostly moaning she thought was her imagination was actually coming from somewhere in the house. She rose slowly, her book falling to the floor, and went to the head of the staircase, holding her candle, the flame of which wavered in the draft, sending weird shadows flying up around the walls.

"Who's there?" she called softly.

Again, that unearthly moaning.

Alarmed, and putting all thoughts of ghosts firmly from her mind, Jean thought that some servant might be in pain and walked down the stairs.

Then she realized the moans were coming from the long gallery and remembered the gray lady.

With a trembling hand she opened the door to the long gallery. There, standing in a shaft of moonlight, was the gray lady. Then she appeared to drift forward into the black shadows at the end of the gallery and disappear.

Jean opened her mouth to scream, but no sound came out. She turned away and stumbled up the stairs, making little whimpering sounds of fright. Her steps instinctively took her to the viscount's bedchamber.

She staggered in and then ran to the bed and drew back the curtains. The viscount started up in alarm. "What the deuce . . . !" he began.

And Jean Morrison threw herself straight into his arms.

Chapter Five

"OH, M-MY L-LORD," Jean babbled. "The ghost!"

He hugged her, and the sensations that evoked were singularly pleasant, and so he hugged her closer. "Calmly now," he said. "What ghost?"

"In the long gallery," Jean whispered. "The ghost of the gray lady."

Jean was not wearing any stays. Her body was soft and yielding under his comforting hands which were stroking her back and were now itching to move around to her front. "And what did she look like?" he murmured against her hair, beginning to enjoy himself immensely and wondering whether a comforting kiss would be in order.

But Jean recovered enough to be aware that she was in, or rather on, the viscount's bed and that he was holding her very closely. She extricated herself and stood a little way away from the bed in a shaft of moonlight that showed the viscount clearly the rise and fall of her excellent bosom. "I should not have burst in on you in this hurly-burly way," Jean said shakily. "But I am monstrous frightened."

He sighed a little and swung his legs down from the bed. "Hand me my dressing gown, Miss Morrison. It is there, behind you, on the chair. Light the lamp and we will go and lay your ghost."

Jean fumbled with the tinderbox, striking weak, ineffectual sparks from it while the viscount donned his dressing gown, took the tinderbox from her shaking fingers, and lit the lamp.

He picked it up and said, "Lead the way."

Given courage by his calm manner, Jean walked before him to the long gallery. It was empty. The shafts of moonlight still struck down. She stood in the doorway as he carefully walked the length of it, holding the lamp high and searching about.

"Nothing," he said cheerfully. "And why are you dressed?"

"I was sitting on the landing, on guard," Jean said, "in case the twins tried to go out. And then I heard the moaning."

"And it could not be either of those wretched girls, playing a trick? Did you look in on them before you sat guard?"

"N-no."

"There you are."

"But the ghost was taller than either of them and it just disappeared into thin air."

"Come with me." He led the way up to the twins' bedroom. Jean unlocked the door. The maid had earlier locked it after having put the girls to bed and had given Jean the key. Both were lying asleep.

Jean and the viscount retreated quietly.

"It was the buttered crab at dinner," the viscount said sympathetically. He walked to the landing. "And here is your book. Tut-tut, Miss Morrison. Such horrors are enough to make anyone see ghosts. Off to bed with you. But should you hear any moaning again, come to me first."

"I wish he wouldn't interfere!" Amanda said crossly when she heard all was silent outside again.

"But she was frit enough. We'll give her another haunting tomorrow night."

"She'll lock us in," Clarissa pointed out.

"So? We have a duplicate key."

"But if she looks in on us and then sits on guard, we can't use the backstairs on the landing as an escape."

"I'll think o' something," Amanda said comfortably. "I always do."

Jean found it almost impossible to look the viscount in the face the next day. She kept remembering the feel of his arms around her. She blushed furiously when she considered he might have thought she had invented the ghost in order to throw herself at him.

She grew hot and then cold when he came near her; her body was acting strangely, full of stabbing pains and sweet yearning. By dinnertime she felt she could not bear it any longer and miserably asked to be excused, explaining she did not feel well.

She went early to bed, and after tossing and turning for an hour, she eventually fell asleep.

Jean awoke three hours later, conscious that there was someone in her room. "Who's there?" she cried.

"It is I, Hunterdon" came the viscount's voice. "Rouse yourself, Miss Morrison. There is moaning coming from the long gallery. The ghost walks again."

Jean shrank back against the pillows as he lit the candle beside her bed. "Perhaps, my lord, you might go yourself to investigate."

"No, Miss Morrison, I think you should be there. Come!"

She climbed reluctantly down from her high bed and pulled on a wrapper.

Together they walked down to the long gallery. There in front of them was the ghost. It walked to the end of the gallery and disappeared in the blackness. The viscount, holding the candle high, walked to the end as well and stood frowning. There was nothing but a sofa in front of a lacquered cabinet on high, spindly legs. He set the candle in its stick on the floor and pulled the sofa forward. Then he slid the cabinet to one side on the polished floorboards.

"Come here, Miss Morrison," he said over his shoulder.

Jean approached him. He held up the candle. The cabinet and sofa had been hiding a narrow door.

"That's how it was done," he said, amused. "Your ghost rolled under the sofa and under the cabinet and through this door held open by an accomplice. I should guess that this place is a warren of passages and stairs. Now, for our revenge on those brats."

"Can it really be them? Betty would lock them in."

"And I am sure they have a duplicate key."

"So . . . so what are you going to do?"

"What are *we* going to do. Do you know, on reflection, I think we are just going to ignore the whole thing. Do not lock their room anymore or keep guard on them. If you ignore them, they will not try any more tricks. It is high time they became interested in themselves as women."

"At fifteen years!"

"Never too late to begin, Miss Morrison. I shall hold a ball. Perhaps the prospect of ball gowns and beaux will turn their minds in a more civilized direction."

"I will do my best. But they need a dancing master. They would not try to dance well with me."

"I will endeavor to find one. Do you like balls, Miss Morrison?"

"I do not know, my lord, never having been to one."

"Poor Miss Morrison. You shall dance at mine."

"That would not be correct, my lord, and would occasion comment."

He was irritated. "Oh, excellent and moral Miss Morrison. Do you not wish to have some fun?"

"Oh, yes, my lord." Jean looked steadily at him. "But I must consider my future. Once the girls are of age, my work here will be finished. It will become necessary to find new employ. If I behave correctly in front of the county, then I may have hopes of obtaining employment in the future with one of the local families. If I am bold enough to dance, then I will be considered unsuitable."

He stood looking down at her. It had been very pleasant holding her close. She probably danced like an angel. He smiled at her suddenly. "It will be a costume ball, a masked ball, Miss Morrison. Nothing wrong in you dancing at such an affair."

Jean took a slow breath and her eyes shone. "It would be wonderful. You have no idea how irritating it is to have been trained in the steps of all the dances, even the waltz, and never to have danced them, except with Miss Tiggs."

"Miss Tiggs?"

"My governess."

"So do not worry about your charges. They will be so excited about the prospect of a costume ball that they will forget to try to escape at night to eat chocolates!"

To Jean's surprise, the twins did indeed seem elated at the prospect of the ball and talked endlessly of their costumes. Not only that, but with their amazing knowledge of who was resident in the neighborhood, they said they knew of a dancing master, lately come to St. Giles.

The viscount said cynically that there was not enough scope in a market town to keep a dancing master in shoes, but Amanda said this one was resident at The George, a gentleman, and reported to be only on a brief stay. He was a French émigré, Jacques Perdu.

"What an odd name," Jean exclaimed. "*Perdu* means 'lost.' But it might answer and he could converse in French with Amanda and Clarissa to improve their accent."

"The English accent is in need of improving first," the viscount said dryly. "Very well, I will ride to St. Giles today and look him over."

The viscount was pleasurably surprised by Mr. Perdu. He was an elegant young Frenchman who said his parents had escaped the Terror and were now resident in London. He himself had been visiting friends and had stayed on in Dorset in order to enjoy the English countryside before returning to London. He danced for the viscount to demonstrate how well he knew all the steps. He was a small man with an acrobat's figure, curly black hair, an olive skin, and sparkling black eyes. When offered the temporary post of dancing master, he accepted gracefully. "The Misses Courtney have an excellent governess, or, rather, companion," said

89

the viscount, "but it is always better to have a gentleman teach them the steps. You will find they lack manners and elegance. Do your best. I do not expect miracles. Just make sure they know enough not to cripple their partners."

Both Jean and the viscount expected that the twins would try to make the dancing master's life hell, but to their surprise, both Amanda and Clarissa seemed almost in awe of the little Frenchman and both desperately tried to please him.

"I feel quite put out," Jean confided to the viscount. "I am obviously of the wrong sex."

"Don't think on't," the viscount urged. "Take a holiday and concentrate on your own costume. Schoolbooks can be put aside until after the ball. You will notice they have given up haunting. What do you think of the gardens at the back of the house? Quite a jungle."

"It's a pity it's the back of the house," Jean said, "for there are the most beautiful views of the sea."

His eyes lit up. "No reason why we cannot turn this architectural horror back to front. But after the ball. I suppose I must include my cousin Basil among the invitations. It is a wonder he has not called before this. If he can find aught amiss with the upbringing of the girls, then he can write to the lawyers and try to get the estates moved to him."

Jean looked at him uneasily. "Do the twins know this?"

"Yes."

"What if they meet Mr. Devenham and decide they prefer him to you? They could make all sorts of mischief."

"They're happy enough with their Frenchman, and I'll make sure Basil is kept away from them."

Jean decided to walk through the terraced gardens at the back and see if she could come up with some idea of how they might be cleared and landscaped. That way she could have yet another opportunity to talk to the viscount alone. She was thankful, or so she told herself severely, that all those silly feelings she had briefly had about him had died away. It was—again she lectured herself—because she had no other adults to talk to except the servants.

The day was hazy and warm. A few brave roses struggled through the undergrowth of weeds and hung their heavy-scented heads over the mossy paths. Instead of taking the path that led straight down to the beach, Jean turned along one that led to the left. Briars tore at her skirts, and she would have turned back had she not seen a glimpse of the low roof of what looked like a folly, or summerhouse, so she forged on. A sea gull screamed somewhere nearby, and then came the call of another, reminding her of that day when she had found the cave.

She heard a twig crack and looked back along the path which was like a green tunnel. Perhaps it might be better to return to the house and just tell the viscount that she thought there was an interesting folly, or summerhouse, in the grounds. But perhaps, just a little farther on to get a look at it. She impatiently stepped over a fallen log.

Suddenly, something struck her savagely on the back of the head, and she fell unconscious among the undergrowth.

The viscount was looking anxiously for Jean Morrison. The twins had told him they planned to attend his costume ball as fairies. He thought Amanda in particular with those scowling black eyebrows would look ridiculous. Why couldn't they go as demons? That would be more in keeping with their looks and personality. Miss Morrison must dissuade them. But where was Miss Morrison? The servants said they had last seen her walking around to the back of the house. He remembered suggesting she look at the gardens, and headed that way.

He was about to follow the path down to the beach when he heard a faint moaning coming from the left. He wondered at first whether the twins were playing a trick, but faintly from behind him he heard the sound of the pianoforte as Mr. Perdu played to the girls' dancing. He hurried along the path to the left.

He heard the moaning sounds again and then saw a neat foot and excellent ankle sticking out into the mossy path from the undergrowth. He ran along and found Jean lying moaning, her face ashen white.

He scooped her up into his arms, exclaiming, "What happened?"

"Something hit me on the back of the head," she said faintly. He carried her along the path and out of the wilderness of the garden, laid her gently down on a patch of grass, and examined the back of her head. "A nasty blow," he said. "We had best get the physician to have a look at you."

He picked her up again and walked toward the house, cradling her against his chest.

Followed by an anxious Mrs. Moody and two maids, he carried her up to her bedchamber and laid her gently on her bed. "I'll leave you to undress her," he said to the housekeeper. "The physician will be here shortly."

Downstairs again, he sent a footman off to St. Giles to bring the physician and then walked back to the gardens to where he had found Jean. There was a broken branch on the path. He picked it up and examined it. There were a few red hairs and some blood stuck to it. He looked up. There above him was a rotten tree and a break showing where the branch had fallen off. That should solve the mystery, he mused. And yet, surely the falling branch would have crashed into some of the tangling of branches below before falling onto Jean's head. On the other hand, who would have reason to strike her down? He shook his head. He had been listening to too many fantastic tales in the evenings.

The physician—to Jean's relief—said she did not need any stitches. Stitching would have meant shaving a part of her head. She was told to stay in bed and rest quietly. At first Jean was glad to comply, for she felt very weak. But after two days she felt much stronger, and it was maddening to hear all the preparations for the ball already going on— although the ball was not to be held for another month.

She roused herself, looking forward to seeing the viscount at dinner. But the lord lieutenant of the county and his lady had come to call and had been pressed by the viscount to stay for dinner. The newly refurbished morning room next to the drawing room was to be used as a dining room for Jean, the dancing master, and the twins. Jean felt the gulf between herself and the viscount widening. The more people he met socially, the less he would expect her company at table. She felt almost resentful of the presence of the dancing master, feeling had he not now been resident at the castle, perhaps she and the girls might just have been allowed to the dinner table proper.

Mr. Perdu chattered away to Amanda and Clarissa, promising them both dances at the ball. He had only a very slight French accent.

He then turned his attention to Jean. "And what will you be wearing by way of a costume, Miss Morrison?"

"I have not really thought about it. I suppose I had better decide on something before it is too late."

He tilted his head on one side and looked at her consideringly. "With your color of hair, miss, I would suggest Queen Elizabeth."

"A good idea, but too elaborate a costume to be made in such a short time."

"There is such a one. There is a chest of clothes in the attics dating back to when this really was a castle, and well preserved in camphor, too."

"And what were you doing in the attics?" Jean asked curiously.

He smiled. "The ladies and I became tired of dancing and hopping and so we went to explore. There is also a chest of costumes. The ladies have chosen two Turkish ones which the seamstress is altering."

"You might have told me," Jean said to Amanda.

Amanda scowled horribly. "If you hadn't been poking your nose into the shrubbery and getting hit on the head, I might have."

"Mind your manners," Jean snapped, and Mr. Perdu said smoothly, "That is no way to talk to your governess." His black eyes mocked Jean. "A governess of distinction, too."

The twins exchanged smiles with him. Jean felt uneasy. There was an odd conspiratorial air about the dancing master and the two girls. He was young and undeniably attractive, and the girls could expect good dowries. She hoped he was not ambitious enough to try to woo one of them. The viscount had told her to take a holiday from the schoolroom and to leave the twins to their dancing lessons, but she felt she was losing her control over them. Still, the dancing master was to be employed only until the ball. Now she longed for the ball to be over and done with so she might return to those relaxed intimate evenings, dining with the viscount and reading to him and the girls after dinner.

When dinner was over she asked to be taken to the attics to inspect the costumes. In the chest she found an Elizabethan gown of green silk, heavily encrusted with gold. It should be easy to get a ruff to go with it, she thought, for ruffs had just come back into fashion. There was also a farthingale. Then the twins led her to the seamstress's little room to examine their Turkish costumes which Jean was relieved to notice were modest enough, not being the genuine article but having obviously been designed for some earlier costume ball.

After that evening it was somehow understood that Jean should take her meals with the dancing master and the twins. The viscount was always busy. There were callers every day now. The Pembertons had not reappeared, although they, with Toad Basil, had been invited to the ball.

An orchestra was to play in the long gallery and carts were arriving with rout chairs to be put along the walls of the hall where the dance was to be held.

Then the viscount's friends arrived back from London to stay, and their presence as guests in the house put a further social barrier between Jean and the viscount. And then, just before the ball more friends of the viscount's descended, lords and ladies and their entourages and their hopeful daughters. Jean found herself being squeezed more and more into the background.

She was about to pass the time by putting some final stitches in the Elizabethan costume she was altering, but as she made her way up the main staircase, a Lady Conham and her daughter, Eliza, walked past her as if she were invisible, talking animatedly. "Are you sure you want to go to this ball as Queen Elizabeth, Mama?" the daughter said. "I have heard that Lady Pemberton has chosen just that costume."

"There may be many duplicates," Lady Conham said placidly, "and there is no time now to change."

Jean bit her lip. She did not want to be just another Elizabeth at that ball. She ran up to the attics and feverishly began to search through the chests of costumes. She took out a pretty blue silk ball gown in the style of 1750. It had been wrapped in tissue paper and was still in good condition, and hanging on the wall of the attic was a hoop that could go under it. She could powder her dreadful red hair and go as who? Marie Antoinette? Well, that might be in bad taste. Just as a gentlewoman. She carried the costume to her room and tried it on. It fitted perfectly, although the low square neckline cried out for some jewelry.

She dressed in her own clothes again and walked

down the stairs. All the guests present knew Jean Morrison was nothing other than a governess despite her fashionable gown, and they walked past her as if she did not exist.

"Miss Morrison!" She turned and looked up at the viscount. "I have not seen much of you of late. You are looking thoughtful. Have your charges tried to murder you again?"

Jean smiled. "No, my lord. I was thinking about my costume. I was going to go as Queen Elizabeth but I overheard Lady Conham saying *she* was going as Queen Elizabeth, and Lady Pemberton, too. I found a costume in the attics of about sixty years ago which is vastly pretty. But I do not have any jewelry and the ladies of that period wore such a lot."

"There is a box of the stuff in my room," he said. "The Courtney jewelry. It may be rather dirty, as I don't think any of it has been worn for some considerable time. But come and look at it."

He walked up the stairs beside her, talking companionably, and once more Jean passed Lady Conham and her daughter, but this time they did not ignore her but stared at her with hard, speculative eyes.

Once in his dressing room next to his bedchamber, the viscount lifted down a heavy metal box from the top of the wardrobe. He fished a small key out of a drawer on a table and unlocked the box. "What color is your gown?" he asked.

"Blue—blue silk," Jean said, looking wonderingly down at the sparkling jewels.

"Pity. With eyes like yours it should have been green. Here we are! Is this not magnificent? I have never really looked closely at these jewels before."

He held up a heavy sapphire necklace, sapphires set in circles of tiny diamonds.

Jean looked at it longingly. "It is too fine for a governess."

"Not governess, companion, and no one will know who you are, for you will be masked. Turn around and let's try it on."

Jean did as she was bid, trembling slightly as his hands brushed against the back of her neck. "Now look in the mirror!"

He turned her toward a long pier glass. Her gown was a modest one of pure white muslin, but the neck was fairly low and the sapphires gleamed like blue fire against the whiteness of her neck.

He was holding her lightly by the shoulders, standing behind her as she faced the glass.

"Why," he said in a voice tinged with wonder, "you are beautiful!"

And he bent his head and kissed her gently on the side of the neck.

She shivered and took a step forward. "My lord!"

"I am sorry," he said quickly. "But for a moment I forgot who you were. Do not look so pale and frightened, Miss Morrison. Do I look the kind of man who would seduce a governess?"

Jean dumbly shook her head.

"And will you forgive me and make use of this necklace?"

Jean nodded.

"Then off with you, Miss Morrison, and do forget my lapse from good taste."

Jean undid the heavy catch of the necklace and then went quickly from the room, clutching it in her hand. She wanted to cry. She wanted to break things. Above all, she wanted to be a rich young lady who could stand a chance with the beautiful viscount.

She firmly reminded herself of her duties and went to the drawing room. The piano had been carried back there and the carpet rolled up. But the dancing master and the twins were sitting by the window, their heads together, whispering fiercely.

"You will never learn to dance at this rate," Jean exclaimed.

Mr. Perdu immediately leapt to his feet. "Sure, and weren't we just having a well-earned rest," he said merrily. "Now, young ladies, let us show Miss Morrison how well you waltz! Miss Morrison, play for us."

Jean sat down at the piano, mechanically selected a piece of waltz music, and started to play. She had been sure that Mr. Perdu's first sentence had been spoken in an Irish accent, although when he had asked her to play, his voice had reverted to his usual French one.

She twisted around as she played, saying, "It is very hard to play and see what you are doing."

"Then stop," Mr. Perdu said gaily, "and we'll move the piano."

Jean stood aside while he manhandled it around to face the room. He was, she noticed, despite his small stature, extremely strong. She began to play again. Amanda and Clarissa danced beautifully, their short, squat bodies actually achieving a certain grace.

When they had finished their demonstration, she said warmly, "Excellent. You have done wonders, sir."

"Miss Morrison is going to the ball as Queen Elizabeth," Amanda said.

Jean opened her mouth to tell them about her change of plans and then closed it again. She felt strangely guilty about that necklace. It was not correct that the viscount should lend such precious gems to a mere governess.

The night of the ball rushed upon them. The days leading up to it seem to have moved slowly, but suddenly here it was. Mrs. Moody, the housekeeper, resplendent in a new black silk gown, bustled about, seeing that all the bedchambers were aired and ready for any who wished to change into their costumes after arrival. A little-used anteroom off the hall had been furnished with a dressing table and boxes of powder and pins. Betty was to sit there in attendance, collecting the cloaks of the arriving ladies, and ready to help with torn hems or other disasters.

Jean put on her costume, spreading the blue silk skirts over the wide hoop. She back-combed her hair and arranged it up on her head before powdering it with some scented powder she had found in the attics. She placed a black patch high on one cheekbone and then put the heavy necklace around her neck. A stranger looked back at her from the glass, an elegant, poised stranger. She picked up a blue silk mask she had made and tied it on. Just this one evening she was going to pretend to be a lady. Would he remember to dance with her? There were so many pretty ladies present, marriageable ladies. He should not have kissed her. But, oh, what would it be liked if he kissed her on the mouth? Jean shivered and tried to banish that wicked dream from her head. But it persisted, and she gave herself up to it, finally realizing with a start that the ball had started and that she should collect her charges and take them downstairs.

She went to the twins' room and found it empty. They had gone downstairs without her. She retreated to her own room, suddenly shy. To go down to the ball with the twins was one thing, but to go down on her own was another. She had never been to a ball before.

The sounds of a waltz filtered upstairs. She should be there, in his arms, dancing the waltz, but she seemed frozen with fright, unable to move.

"But if you don't move," said a jeering voice in her head, "you will have nothing to remember when you are a tired old maid."

She picked up a painted fan and hung it over one wrist, edged her wide skirts through the bedroom door, and made for the stairs.

The waltz had finished and the cotillion was about to begin. The viscount was talking to several costumed guests. He was dressed as a gentleman of the last century; pink silk coat embroidered with gold, white silk kneebreeches, white silk stockings with gold clocks, and a ruffled shirt. His hair was powdered. Someone next to him gave an exclamation and looked up. Then everyone seemed to be staring up at the newcomer descending the staircase.

The viscount let out a low whistle of appreciation. Jean Morrison was walking down the stairs, her head held high and the necklace blazing at her throat. He walked forward, bowed low, and held out his hand. "My dance, princess," he said.

There was a buzz of speculation. Princess! He had said princess!

Basil Devenham in a Puritan costume sourly

watched his rival. "Who is that lady who is partnering Hunterdon in the cotillion?" he asked Lady Pemberton.

Lady Pemberton, dressed as Queen Elizabeth, looked at him in a dazed way and then slid off her rout chair and fell onto the floor. Her red wig toppled from her head. Basil bent over her and then exclaimed, "She is dead drunk, I think!"

Lord Pemberton tried to rouse his wife by gently slapping her wrists, but she slept on. He was still eager to try to secure Hunterdon for one of his daughters and knew they would never forgive him if he took them from the ball. So he solved the situation by having his wife put in his carriage and borne off home with her maid to accompany her while he and his daughters stayed.

Then Lady Conham, also a Queen Elizabeth, collapsed in the middle of the ballroom. The dancing was brought to a halt while the unfortunate lady was carried upstairs to a bedchamber.

The viscount's eyes ranged over the ballroom. Amanda and Clarissa were both there, a pair of small, squat Turks, but behaving quite prettily.

"Walk with me," he said to Jean. When they had moved a little way away from the guests, he asked, "Did the girls know of your change of costume?"

"No."

"And so two Queen Elizabeths in red wigs promptly fall unconscious. We will see what the physician has to say about Lady Conham when he arrives, but it is my belief that the two ladies were drugged, and it is also my belief that the twins were trying to get you out of the way for the evening."

"But why?"

"I do not know. But keep a close eye on them.

They have not yet recognized you with your powdered hair and mask, so introduce yourself to them but do not drink anything at all."

The twins looked at Jean in a fury when she revealed who she was. "You was supposed to be Queen Elizabeth?" Amanda said hotly.

"And is that why two Queen Elizabeths have been taken ill?" Jean studied them, wishing their faces were not masked.

"Nothing to do with us. Here's your next partner."

Jean found a young man at her elbow soliciting her to dance. Amanda and Clarissa were claimed by their partners. Jean made sure she was in the same set for a country dance as the twins. She watched them closely as she danced and knew they were aware of it, for they had lost their grace of movement and their hot, angry little black eyes stared at her resentfully.

When everyone went in at last to supper, Jean made sure she was sitting next to the girls. There was no sign of the dancing master, and she asked them where Mr. Perdu was. "Upstairs," Amanda said, and added nastily, "*He* knows his place."

But then Jean became distracted. She also had a clear view of the viscount, and he was flirting with a very young lady seated near him. He was a born flirt, thought Jean miserably, and kissing governesses on the neck meant as little to him as a casual kiss to a tavern wench. He looked across at her, and she immediately stared down at her plate of untouched food.

After supper her hand was claimed for the waltz, not by the viscount, but by Basil Devenham, who was stiff and formal in his Puritan clothes. He introduced himself and begged to know Jean's name, but Jean had no intention of letting the viscount's rival know she was a governess. He might tell the lawyers that Hunterdon's governess was unseemly gowned and bedecked in the Courtney jewels, and the lawyers might jump to the conclusion that she was the viscount's mistress. So she laughed and said he would find out when the unmasking took place. But he questioned her closely about the viscount, and Jean said tartly that he was a good influence on the Misses Courtney and a good landlord, which made Basil fall moodily silent, much to Jean's relief. But dealing with Basil had been a strain. After the dance was over he offered to fetch her a glass of lemonade and went off to get it. She saw with relief that the twins were still in evidence. Basil returned with the glass, stumbled, and spilled most of the contents over her gown.

Jean brushed aside his apologies and decided to go up to her room and sponge the gown. Amanda and Clarissa were involved in a lengthy quadrille. In her room she quickly removed the stain and made her way out. Surely the viscount would dance a waltz with her, just once.

There was an oil lamp burning on the landing. Then Jean noticed that a cabinet had been pushed to one side, revealing a door.

Startled, she hurried back to the ballroom, her eyes scanning the dancers.

Of Amanda and Clarissa there was no sign.

The viscount was talking with his London friends. She crossed to him, drew him aside, and told him about the secret door and the twins' absence.

"Show me," he said. "It would be like them to

perpetrate some awful mischief while Basil is here."

They walked up the staircase together, Jean conscious of curious eyes boring into her back.

He looked at the door behind the cabinet and said, "I'd better have a look. And tomorrow I had better get out the blueprints to this place. Too many secret passages for my liking."

"I'm coming with you," Jean said. "Please."

"You'll never get through that narrow door with that hoop."

"Wait!"

Jean ran to her room and tugged off the hoop, unfastened the necklace, hid it under her pillow, looped the silk skirts of her gown over her arm, and ran out to join him.

He had found a candle in a flat stick. "I'll lead the way," he said softly.

A narrow staircase wound down. Suddenly the noise of the orchestra was very loud. "The long gallery," he said, indicating a door. "We should have investigated this staircase before. This is how they escaped up to their rooms after playing ghost."

On down they went, the candle flame suddenly beginning to flicker and bend in a draft of air, and all at once Jean could smell the sea.

Then ahead stood an open door leading out into the wilderness of the gardens at the back of the house. It was clear moonlight outside, so the viscount blew out the candle and stood irresolute.

"The caves," Jean suggested.

"No," he said. "Listen, over to the left."

She listened and then she heard the faint sound of men's voices and the steady dip and rise of oars.

"That old summerhouse," she said. "It's in that direction."

They hurried along the path Jean had taken when she was struck down. Briars tore at her skirts and she wished she had had the foresight to change into an old gown.

Finally the tangle of woods and bushes ended and there, in a little clearing above the beach, stood a folly, or summerhouse, tangled with ivy. A gleam of light came from inside.

They crept up to the window and looked in. Through the door, men were unloading barrels and boxes under the direction of Mr. Perdu while Amanda and Clarissa looked on.

"We expects good payment for this," Amanda said clearly.

"You'll be paid," Perdu said, if that was his name, for his accent was now pure Irish. "One more shipload tomorrow. Bring the lights down to the beach as usual, girls, and guide them in."

The viscount took Jean's arm in a strong grip and drew her away from the window and back into the shrubbery.

"Smugglers," Jean said, her face white. "They have been aiding and abetting smugglers."

Smugglers were not romantic figures. Smugglers threw excisemen off cliffs and tortured to death any who betrayed them. "And Perdu is their leader."

"What a fool I have been," the viscount said bitterly. "What a naive fool. So they conveniently knew a dancing master! How they must have laughed behind our backs."

"What shall we do?" Jean asked urgently. "Call out the militia, the excisemen?"

"Not yet," he said. "Walk back to the house with

me. If we are caught, we will be killed. If Amanda and Clarissa are convicted of smuggling, I will lose everything. The lawyers would decide I was not a proper guardian. If I say they had probably been smuggling for some time, they would laugh at me. What! Two little girls! And everything would go to Basil. No, there is another shipment tomorrow night. *That* is when the excisemen will find them, but without the girls."

"How do we keep them at home?"

"Do what they did to those Queen Elizabeths. The physician who attended Lady Conham says he is persuaded she was suffering from nothing more than a strong dose of some opiate. Now we shall return to the ball as if nothing has happened."

"My gown is ruined," Jean said mournfully.

He laughed. "Only Jean Morrison could fall upon a smuggler's lair and still worry about her appearance."

Back in her room Jean changed into the Elizabethan costume and went back downstairs. After half an hour the twins reappeared, looking smug. Jean could have screamed at them.

And then the viscount asked her to waltz and, for a brief spell, she moved in his arms and forgot about the twins, about perils, about smugglers, seeing the faces of the other guests only as a blur, wishing she could dance with him till the end of time. All too soon it was over. At the unmasking she slipped away and went upstairs. If she took her mask off, Lord Pemberton and his daughters would recognize her and create a scandal. The secret door, she noticed, was closed.

She changed into a morning gown and sat by the window for a long time, listening to the sweet music drifting up through the open window, wondering if the viscount was still flirting, hoping he had enjoyed that dance with her just a fraction as much as she had enjoyed it. Then there came sounds of the resident guests mounting the stairs followed by the rumble of departing carriages outside. When the last sound had died away, she rose and went downstairs again. The viscount was preparing to go out. He had changed into riding dress.

"I cannot sleep until I have told the authorities about our smugglers," he said. "Go to sleep, Miss Morrison. For you will have a deal of work to do tomorrow to keep an eye on that precious pair."

"They are horrible," Jean said with a shudder. "Do you not long for the days when you were a free man?"

He looked at her in dawning surprise. "Faith, I must confess I have grown to love my life here. I live now for the day when those brats will be off my hands. This is a terrible and shocking business, Miss Morrison, and I would dearly love to get that precious pair arrested with the other criminals, but I refuse now to forfeit my inheritance. Well, the ball was a great success, but I am weary of all the company."

Jean looked up at him anxiously. "How am I going to drug the girls without alerting Perdu?"

"Do you think he will have the gall to show his face tomorrow?"

"Of course. He does not know he has been discovered."

"I'll think of something. To bed, Miss Morrison. And sweet dreams." His blue eyes teased her, and he raised her hand to his lips.

Jean snatched her hand away. "Are you never

done flirting, my lord?" she demanded harshly, burst into tears, and stumbled away from him.

He watched her go in amazement and then shrugged. She was not made of iron, and he should have realized the shock of finding out that her charges were smugglers would overset her.

Chapter Six

JEAN SLEPT VERY LITTLE. She told Mrs. Moody and Dredwort to report to her if the twins stepped out of doors. By early afternoon she felt exhausted. She looked in at the girls, but they were both still asleep. The servants reported that Mr. Perdu was in his room, packing.

By four o'clock the viscount returned, his face grim. He called Jean to the library and sank down heavily into a chair, saying, "Well, all is ready for this evening. We should catch the lot of them red-handed. The authorities have been trying to catch them for the past two years. They have committed murder and torture. I must warn you not to betray any knowledge of what you know to Perdu, if that is his name, which I doubt, by any look or action. Now, how are Amanda and Clarissa to be drugged?"

"I am worried about that," Jean said, "for if they fall into a drugged sleep, Perdu will be alerted. Perhaps I might find something in the stillroom to make them sick, just for the night. They are always stuffing themselves with sweetmeats when they can get them. I suppose those expensive chocolates came from France."

"Oh, undoubtedly. But we cannot question the

girls until all this is over. I would dearly like to know how they started in this evil trade. I have a feeling they knew Perdu well before he even appeared here masquerading as a dancing master. Also, when this is over, there is the question of what to do with them."

A hand seemed to clutch Jean's heart and she looked at him wide-eyed. "What do you mean, my lord?"

"Why, only that they cannot stay here, polluting this house with their evil games."

Jean attempted a light note. "I should be, in that case, without work."

He regarded her thoughtfully. "Ye-es," he agreed. "Then what, Miss Morrison? Would your aunt have you back again?"

Jean thought of all the drudgery of her life should Mrs. Delmar-Richardson decide to take her back, and a lump rose in her throat. "I should think that is highly unlikely."

"Well, I shall just need to find something for you," he said vaguely.

"Thank you," Jean said in a low voice. The library door opened and Eliza Conham sailed in followed by the viscount's three friends. She stopped short at the sight of Jean.

"Servant problems?" she asked lightly.

Jean curtsied to the viscount and left the room quickly. As she crossed the hall, she could hear the light chatter of Eliza's voice and the viscount's answering laugh. If the twins were sent away somewhere, what would become of her? She would need to look for another position. She gazed around the great hall, now tastefully furnished with statuary, elegant chairs, paintings, and bowls of flowers. She had come to love this odd monstrosity of a house. From outside came the cheerful talk of the gardeners and laborers who were transforming the gardens. It would have been wonderful to stay long enough to see all the improvements finished.

For the first time Jean experienced a spasm of real hatred for her charges. Why could they not have been normal little misses instead of two wanton criminals?

She went down to the stillroom and asked the maid who was working there if she might look around. The maid bobbed a curtsy and left. Jean studied a large recipe book, turning the pages until she came to Emetic Tartar. "Causes a burning pain in the region of the stomach, vomiting, and great purging. It has not often been known to destroy life."

She did not want them devasted, only too ill to go out. She searched the shelves until she found a small blue glass jar containing the tartar crystals. But what to put the emetic in? Something, she thought, that they were forbidden to eat. Then she remembered that in the hampers of delicacies that had arrived from London for the supper at the ball had been boxes of chocolates. Amanda and Clarissa had been told firmly to leave them alone. But what if they were to come across some?

Jean went out of the stillroom and asked a maid to fetch her some chocolates if there were any left. The maid brought back a large box that was half-full.

Jean dismissed her and then carefully inserted a tiny amount of the crystals, which she first powdered, into each chocolate. With a warm knife she carefully repaired the sweets so that there was no sign they had been tampered with. Then she fetched a tazza from the kitchen and arranged the chocolates on it. She did not want to be seen carrying the tazza herself, so she handed the glass dish to a footman and told him to take it up to the drawing room. She experienced a momentary pang. What if the viscount's guests helped themselves to the chocolates? On the other hand, they usually congregated in the library or in the Green Saloon, the drawing room because of the dancing lessons being regarded as an extension to the schoolroom.

She waited for a half hour and then went up to the drawing room, hearing the sound of laughter as she approached. She opened the door. Mr. Perdu was there with the twins. He jumped up when he saw her, crying, "Why, here is our beautiful Miss Morrison!"

Jean's eyes went straight to the tazza. All the chocolates were still there. She was not worried about Perdu eating any of them, for he had already claimed a distaste for sweetmeats, but she could not understand why the girls had not touched them. On the other hand, if she *forbade* them to touch them . . .

"Chocolates!" she exclaimed. "What are those things doing here? You are not to touch them!"

"We haven't touched 'em," Amanda said. "We're keeping ourselves slim and beautiful," and she threw Mr. Perdu a flirtatious look while Clarissa simpered. Jean's heart sank. Of course the girls were enamored of the smuggler. Still, it was worth a try. She picked up the tazza. "I shall take temptation out of your way, however." Then she pretended to hear something and put the glass dish back down. "I think I hear Mrs. Moody calling. I shall return shortly. *Don't touch even one choco-late!*"

"You know something," Amanda said, greedily eyeing the chocolates, "that one fancies herself as mistress o' the house. We're the ladies here, not her. Demme, I'm going to have one."

She picked the largest one and chewed it appreciatively. Perdu laughed. "I always like a lady who's a cozy armful." That was enough for Clarissa, who took one as well.

Jean found Mrs. Moody and engaged her in conversation, asking her how long the guests were going to stay while all the time waiting tensely to hear if anything was happening in the drawing room. And then Perdu came running up.

"My ladies are ill," he cried.

Jean hurried to the drawing room, followed by Mrs. Moody. She was glad when she saw that they had eaten half the chocolates that she had put only a tiny drop in each, for, as it was, the twins looked deathly ill. Maids were called along with Betty, the lady's maid, to take them to their room and the physician was sent for. He diagnosed food poisoning and purged the twins further and then dosed them with laudanum until, by evening, they were both fast asleep.

The viscount was entertaining his guests at dinner, and so she could not tell him of her success. She herself was forced to dine with Perdu. She was suddenly very glad he did not like chocolates. If he had fallen ill as well, who would wave the lights on the beach to guide the smugglers in? And then how would they be easily caught?

"You are very pensive tonight," Perdu remarked.

"I am tired," Jean said. "I did not get very much sleep last night. I did not see you at the ball."

"As I am only the dancing master," he said with mock humility, "I considered it better to stay abovestairs.

"How is your head now?" he asked. "I gather a branch fell on you."

His eyes were teasing, and all at once Jean was sure that one of his men had struck her down. She replied calmly that she felt well and ate steadily, managing to maintain a flow of light conversation to hide her loathing and distaste for the man.

At last dinner was over. She retired to her room, rang the bell, and told the footman who answered its summons to ask the viscount if she could speak to him.

The footman returned to say he awaited her in the drawing room. Jean was glad she had taken the rest of those chocolates and thrown them away before anyone else could eat them.

He rose to meet her as she entered. He was finely dressed in an impeccable evening coat and breeches. He looked as if he did not have a care in the world.

"When did Perdu say he was leaving, my lord?" Jean asked.

"Tomorrow morning, of course. He had the impertinence to ask for double the fee promised him, so I told him I would pay him in the morning, by which time he should be well and truly locked up."

"And what do we do?"

"You do nothing this evening, Miss Morrison, except go to bed. There will be a whole army down at that summerhouse."

"Do your guests know anything of this?'

"Of course not. I have told them not to be disturbed by any sounds of shooting in the night, that the wilderness of garden at the back is overrun with rabbits and that the servants are clearing them."

"In the middle of the night? Will they believe that?"

He smiled. "They have all drunk so much, they will believe anything. I also made up my mind to shorten their stay by saying that the builders were moving in tomorrow. My poor friends from London are the only ones who are upset. They keep saying they are tired of making the long journey, only to be sent away again. They had planned to stay for two months."

"And so what is to become of the Misses Courtney?"

"I shall deal with that problem when I have dealt with the present one. Go to bed, Miss Morrison."

Jean curtsied and left. She looked in on the twins. They were sleeping heavily. She closed their door softly and went to her own room. She was too strung up to go to bed. She settled herself in a chair and tried to read, but she listened all the while for sounds of shooting.

At last she could not bear the suspense any longer. She went out to the landing, moved aside the cabinet, and opened the door to the secret stairway. She walked down it, holding a candle which she extinguished as soon as she reached the garden.

The night was very black and still. She stayed where she was at the entrance to the secret stairway, knowing that the gardens must be crawling with men waiting for the smugglers.

Then she heard the harsh cry of a sea gull far away and the answering cry from somewhere on the beach in the direction of the summerhouse. Silence again. The moon moved out from behind a cloud, silvering the leaves of a bush near her, lighting up the twisting path where she had been struck down. Then she heard faintly the smooth rise and dip of oars. Perdu would be on the beach, waving a lantern to guide the men in.

She could hear men's voices now, the scrape of a boat's keel on the sand, an occasional grunt as barrels and kegs were lifted ashore.

Then silence again, a silence so complete that she began to wonder if no one had turned up to arrest the smugglers.

The moon slid behind a cloud again, and all was calm and peaceful.

A great voice shouting "In the King's name!" made her jump. Then the bushes seemed to be alive with men. Jean backed slowly into the passage behind her and fumbled to light the candle. At last she succeeded and was just about to mount the stairs when she heard the sound of running footsteps. She stayed, frozen, at the foot of the stairs.

Perdu darted into the passage, his face glittering with sweat. He was holding a gun. He saw her and his eyes narrowed. "Not a word," he snarled. "Not a murmur. Up the stairs with you."

Jean numbly led the way, cursing herself for her folly. The gun was rammed into her back. When she reached the landing, he told her to go to her room. She thought he was going to lock her in and then make his escape, but he pushed his way in after her and then locked the door. Jean set the candle down on a table, noticing with an odd pride that her hand was steady.

"Now," he said, "you interfering bitch. I see it all. You poisoned my little helpers with those damned chocolates. You brought this on me. Do you know what I do to informers? I roasted a man alive over a spit like an animal a year ago." He gave an ugly laugh. All charm was stripped from him. He looked evil and brutal.

"You aren't French," Jean said. "I don't even think you have ever been a dancing master."

"Oh, I was that, my fine lady, in Dublin some years ago. There's little that the Irish bastard of some English lord can do for a living."

"Are you going to kill me?" Jean asked.

"Not now. You will write a note that you will put onto the outside of your door, saying you are sick and you desire to be left alone. I will hide out here while they scour the countryside for me."

"And if I refuse to write such a note? A shot would be heard, you know."

"I wouldn't waste a bullet on you, you trollop. Strangling's good enough for you. Now, write! And no tricks."

Jean took out her traveling writing case, wishing it contained a knife or gun or something she could use against him. She wrote: "I desire not to be disturbed. I have the vapors, J. Morrison."

She passed it to him. He read it and then ordered her to fasten it on the outside of her door, keeping her covered all the while with the gun as he unlocked the door. Jean wedged the note into the fingerplate.

"What now?" she asked.

"Well, now I think we pass the night pleasantly. You can start by taking your clothes off."

The viscount was cursing the escape of Perdu, the ringleader. They had captured everyone else. He walked into the castle hall, restless and uneasy. He felt he had better check the girls' room, because the more he thought about it, the more he realized Perdu would try to go to ground instead of fleeing across the countryside.

The twins were fast asleep. He checked under their bed and in the wardrobe just to make sure. He found the duplicate key to their door and pocketed it. Then he walked to Jean's room, hoping to find the door open so that he could tell her of the night's adventures. He saw the note and read it. Poor Miss Morrison! He gave a wry smile and turned away. He was halfway down the stairs when it suddenly struck him that Jean Morrison was not the sort of lady to suffer from the vapors. Or even if she did, she would be too proud to say so. And what lady, feeling ill, locked her door?

He ran down to the servants' quarters, grabbed the spare key to Jean's bedroom, went to the library desk, took a pistol from the bottom drawer, and primed it, cursing at the time it took. He ran up the stairs.

Inside her bedroom Jean was backed against the wall, facing her tormentor, who was laughing at her. "You appear to think it a fate worse than death," he jeered. "Come here!"

Jean, her nerves strained to the breaking point, heard a soft footfall in the passage outside. She turned away from him and looked down at the toilet table. Her eyes fell on a bottle of scent she had bought in St. Giles. She gently removed the stopper. Turning back and holding the bottle behind her back, she smiled at Perdu. "Perhaps we could come to an arrangement," she said.

"That's more like it," he said with a grin. He

moved toward her. She heard the key turn in the lock, whipped out the scent bottle, blessing the fact that it had a wide top, and dashed the contents in his face. She darted to one side as he fired blindly. There was an answering report from the doorway, and Perdu fell to his knees, clutching the spreading red stain on his chest as the viscount entered the room.

Jean flew into the viscount's arms, crying, "He was going to rape me. I did not know what to do. Is he dead?"

He gently extricated himself from her clinging arms and knelt down beside Perdu. "Not yet," he said laconically, "but any moment now. I may as well rouse the servants and get them to remove him. I have kept them out of this affair, fearing word of our ambush might get out."

"Do you mind if I leave this room?" Jean asked faintly.

"Of course not. You have been very brave." He bent once more over Perdu. "Yes, quite dead now. Once we have moved this body, you can go to bed."

"Here!" Jean squeaked. "In a room in which killing has taken place!"

"Take your night rail and go to my room." He saw the expression on her face and said quickly, "I shall find another bed somewhere. Did . . . er . . . Perdu molest you in any way?"

Jean shuddered. "No, you came just in time."

"Then off with you. A good night's sleep is what you need."

Jean collected her night things, wondering at his calm, why he did not try to comfort her, for she had been through enough to devastate the strongest female. Then with a pang she realized she was a servant now, and servants were not expected to have feelings any more than the beasts of the field.

She went into his room rather timidly, undressed, and climbed into his large bed. She lay wide awake for a few moments, still shivering with fright, and then she suddenly fell asleep.

Amanda awoke suddenly, sat up, and looked around groggily. Memory came flooding back, and she shook Clarissa awake. "What's the time?" Amanda hissed.

Clarissa struggled out of bed and drew back the curtains. Gray light flooded the room. "Dawn!" Amanda exclaimed. "Too late. Odd's fish, I still feel like death. I'm damned if I'll ever touch a chocolate again."

"Me too," Clarissa wailed, clutching her stomach.

Amanda grabbed her arm. "Listen! There's the deuce of a commotion coming from downstairs."

She pulled on her wrapper. "Let's creep out and see." She tried the door. "Not locked. Didn't bother to lock us in."

Side by side they went to the landing, then down the stairs, and leaned over the banisters so they could see into the hall. The main door was standing open. The viscount was there, talking to a colonel. As they watched, two soldiers appeared, carrying a body which they dragged outside. A red ray from the rising sun shone full on the dead man's face.

"Perdu!" Amanda gasped. "Oh, God in heaven."

Clarissa began to weep and wail. Alerted by the noise, the viscount looked up and saw them, and his face hardened. "Go to your room immediately," he shouted.

Amanda and Clarissa, sobbing and crying, stumbled back up to their room. By the time the viscount called on them, their weeping had stopped and they were sitting in sullen silence.

"Well?" the viscount demanded. "And what have you pair to say for yourselves?"

"How did he die?" Amanda asked.

"Ah, I note you ask *how* did he die, where an innocent person would have asked *why*. I know you were both in league with Perdu. I gather his name is really Brian Magbee, but we will continue to call him Perdu. He is a murderer and torturer as well as a smuggler. Had it not been for the bravery of Miss Morrison, he might have escaped. Now, then, out with it. Why did you help him?"

Clarissa sniffled dismally. "He forced us to do it," Amanda said. "He said he would kill us, else."

"I saw you together, and you were very merry. I would judge you both doted on the scoundrel. I will try another tack. How long have you been engaged in helping the smugglers? No lies now."

"A year," Amanda said sulkily.

"And how did they pay you? Chocolates?"

"Things like that," Amanda said, having no intention of telling him about the gold they had been paid.

"Before you go back to sleep, you will both accompany me to the schoolroom," the viscount said, "and you will write statements to say that you have been involved in smuggling and you will sign them. I will keep them. I will then decide on your futures. I can do as I wish with you, for one bit of trouble from you and I shall send your statements to the lawyers."

* * *

"Stop weeping and moaning," Amanda snapped when they returned from the schoolroom. "We must think what to do. We must get revenge on him and above all on that Morrison creature for killing poor Mr. Perdu."

Amanda then fell silent, remembering the first time they had met Perdu. He had been strolling on the beach and had fallen into conversation with them. He had flattered them and teased them, and then had introduced them to the smuggling haunts. As they were allowed to roam where they wished, Amanda and Clarissa had enjoyed the vulgar company, and subsequently the bribes of money for their services. Both had been in love with Perdu.

"There's one person who must be interested in harming Hunterdon," Amanda said slowly. "Mr. Devenham. If anything happened to us, he'd get the estates and fortune."

"But what can we do?" Clarissa dried her eyes. "Hunterdon will just send those statements to the lawyers."

"Will he?" Amanda looked at her. "Think on't. The lawyer would inform the authorities, as is his duty, and the authorities would want to know why he kept it quiet. He'd be an . . . an accessory. That's it. Without us he'd stand to lose everything." She smiled slowly. "I wonder if Mr. Devenham would settle for half of everything."

"I don't understand," Clarissa said plaintively.

"Look! We disappear. We arrange with Devenham to keep us somewhere. We send a ransom note demanding half of what the Courtney fortune is worth. He has to pay or lose all."

Clarissa looked at her doubtfully. "Wouldn't he

just pack up and leave? Why would he want us back?"

"No, he loves this place now, the house and the peasants. And precious Miss Morrison would get the blame for not taking care of us. And if we get Devenham on our side, we'll get him to spread it around that she's Hunterdon's mistress. Ruin her!"

Clarissa looked at her sister in awe. "I don't know how you think of such wonderful things. I don't, really."

Jean, dressed in her nightgown, cap, and wrapper, emerged sleepily from the viscount's bedchamber just as the departing Lady Conham and her daughter, Eliza, were making their way downstairs. Lady Conham stopped stock-still and raked Jean up and down with a freezing glance. "Disgraceful!" she said, and then with a toss of her head she walked on while Eliza followed, drawing in her skirts as she passed Jean as if any touch might contaminate her.

Jean said after them, "It is not what you think." But both ladies, their backs rigid, descended the stairs.

It was too bad, thought Jean miserably, that she should have been close to being murdered the night before and have to endure being damned as a trollop the morning after. She went to her room and looked in surprise at the clock. Two in the afternoon!

She washed and dressed and went to the twins' room, but it was empty. She hurried to the schoolroom, praying that they had not escaped, but that was deserted as well. Then she heard the faint sound of the piano from the drawing room and hurried downstairs.

She hesitated, her hand on the door. Highland and superstitious, Jean had a sudden dread that she would open the door and find the ghost of Perdu seated at the piano.

But when she went in, Amanda was seated at the keyboard with Clarissa behind her on the long stool. Amanda was playing a simple tune with her right hand that Jean had taught her. Both girls were neatly dressed and their hair was braided.

Jean closed the door. Amanda stopped playing. Both girls stood up and faced Jean.

She saw their downcast faces and the purple shadows under their eyes, and thought, "I had forgotten. They are little more than children."

"Do you know what happened last night?" she demanded.

"Yes," Clarissa whispered, still mourning for Perdu, but her sister was made of sterner stuff.

"We didn't know we were doing anything wrong," Amanda pleaded. "There's a lot of smuggling going on along this coast, and everyone takes something from the smugglers, tea or silk or wine. Mr. Perdu, he made it all seem like a game."

The fact that Amanda was speaking carefully and precisely should have warned Jean that this was a rehearsed speech, but she did so want to believe them, and besides, it was beyond her comprehension, despite all that had gone on before, that two such little girls could be other than sadly misguided.

Amanda remembered Perdu and gave a convincing sob. "We're most terribly sorry, miss, and we're afeard of the hangman."

Jean rushed to them and gathered them in her arms. "There, now. Do not cry. You have been very wicked, yes, but I blame your father for not having controlled you. You have been punished enough. Now Lord Hunterdon wishes to send you away. But surely if you study hard and behave well, he will come about."

Amanda kissed Jean's cheek. "Thank you, miss," she said in a broken voice. "Oh, thank you."

"So," Jean said briskly, "the sun is shining and you are both pale. Put on your bonnets and we will go for a walk."

The viscount met them in the hall as they were leaving. "Where are you going?" he asked Jean.

"Just for a walk. The Misses Courtney are in need of fresh air."

"The Misses Courtney have nothing up with them that death and mutilation would not cure."

The twins threw themselves into Jean's arms, crying, "Save us!"

Jean held them close and stared defiantly over their heads at the viscount. "They were misled, my lord," she said, "and they are truly penitent."

"Miss Morrison, I am very tired," he said. "I am going to bed. But you will not go anywhere without a guard." He saw Dredwort standing in the shadows, listening with interest. "Dredwort! Two of the grooms, Harry and John, to accompany Miss Morrison on her walk, and that lady's maid, Betty, too. In future, she and the young ladies are not to go anywhere unescorted." He turned back to Jean. "I shall talk to you further when I awake."

When he at last settled his head on the pillows, he realized they smelled faintly of rosewater. Of course! Jean Morrison had been in his bed last night. He should have commended her on her extreme bravery. He should have asked after her health. But before he could think of any of the other things he should have done, he had fallen fast asleep.

Jean walked steadily along the beach, the two grooms and the maid behind her, making it very clear it was the governess they were protecting and not her charges, while the twins walked ahead, talking in low voices.

"I think they know about the secrèt staircase," Amanda whispered, "and we're going to be closely watched. We have to get a letter to Devenham. He's probably still at Pembertons. Wait a bit. A letter might fall into the wrong hands. Damn that poxy, murdering governess. Scotch seed of a whore."

"Face like a twat," Clarissa said, and they both sniggered.

"I think I've got it," Amanda said. "We'll behave like model misses, but we have to be ever so affectionate with Morrison. Get her to think we love her and that our bad behavior was caused by lack o' love. She'll fight him to keep us here and he'll do what she wants 'cause he doesn't care much one way or t'other as long as he's left in peace. Then when everything's settled down and we've got her eating out of our hands, we'll say tearfully that locking us in at night shows a lack of trust—a lack of love. Then we'll be able to sneak out, take a couple o' horses from the stables, and ride over to the Pembertons."

"Big place," Clarissa said. "We won't know where to find him."

"True." Amanda kicked a pebble viciously. Then

her face brightened. "The Pembertons' butler, Sanderson, he took tea and wine off of Perdu. Wouldn't want that known, would he?"

"No," Clarissa said. "But we wouldn't want it known that *we* knew that, and Sanderson might be sharp enough to realize it."

"You're getting mightily clever, sis. Right. Try again. We tell Sanderson we'll have a new source. He likes buying cheap, charging his master dear, and pocketing the difference. We'll tell him we're spoony about Devenham and ask him to take a note to him. In it we'll urge Devenham to meet us somewhere between here and St. Giles."

"But will he come?"

" 'Course, silly. Why do you think he's staying so long with Pemberton? Hoping Hunterdon will slip up somehow."

"When do we start hugging and kissing the Scotch fright?"

"Slowly, slowly. Dawning respect and admiration followed by impulsive outbursts of affection."

"You're beginning to talk like Dr. Johnson's dictionary. What's impulsive?"

"Sudden-like."

"Oh."

"Race you to the end of the beach."

Jean watched the flying figures without bothering to follow them. The tide was in and they could not get past the outcrop. She envied them their resilience. Despite the warmth of the day, she felt cold and alone. She would have liked someone to lean on, someone to tell how really frightened she had been. Although she was used to scenes of violence, of bodies rotting on gibbets, the sight of the dying Perdu lying on her bedroom floor seemed imprinted on her brain. But there was no one to care.

She kept the twins out as long as possible so that they should enjoy the best of the day's sunshine before turning reluctantly back to Trelawney Castle. She dreaded going indoors. The great house that she had been beginning to love now seemed a dark place full of horrors.

Mrs. Moody met her in the hall. "If you please, Miss Morrison," the housekeeper said, "his lordship thought you might enjoy a change of bedroom, and so we have taken the liberty of moving your things."

Jean suddenly remembered the necklace she had hidden under her pillow. "Mrs. Moody, Lord Hunterdon lent me some very expensive jewels for the ball and I left them in my bed."

"They are safe, Miss Morrison. I found them myself and took them to his lordship."

Seeing that the maid, Betty, was walking closely behind the girls as they mounted the stairs, Jean followed the housekeeper. The room allotted to her was one of the guest bedrooms. It had a small dressing room and adjoined a private sitting room. It was light and airy with a fine view of the sea through the open windows.

The bed was modern, without posts, but surmounted with a canopy like a crown from which hung curtains of fine lace. There was a nosegay of flowers on the toilet table at the window and a flat red morocco box. Wondering, Jean opened the box, and there was the sapphire necklace with a little card saying "Thank you for your bravery, H."

Mrs. Moody had left. Jean sat down suddenly, her legs shaky. He cared a little. He cared enough to know she would dread sleeping in the room where Perdu had been shot down.

A footman appeared. "His lordship's compliments, miss, and would you join him for dinner in half an hour?"

All Jean's gloom and misery fled. With a feeling that all her troubles were over, she put on her best gown, boldly fastened the sapphires about her neck, and went down to the dining room.

Chapter Seven

THE VISCOUNT ROSE as Jean entered the dining room and surveyed her appreciatively. She was wearing a gown of soft blue jaconet with a fall of lace at the low neck. The sapphires blazed against the whiteness of her skin. "You look very fine," he said as a footman drew out a chair for her. He put up his quizzing glass. "Dear me, that is cotton lace."

"Yes, my lord." Jean suddenly thought: This is ridiculous. We have shared adventure and near-death and yet the first thing he notices about me is that my lace is cotton!

The viscount was a genuine Regency dandy, that peculiar type of aristocrat who was able to concentrate on trivia even in the middle of a war. Jean remembered her father telling her of some lord, who, when in Flanders, suddenly saw what he thought was a rare flower growing in the midst of the carnage. With musket shot tearing about his ears, he bent down and plucked the flower, took a small notebook out of his pocket and a lead pencil, and carefully wrote down place, time, and date when he had found the flower before pressing it in the pages of his notebook and then recommencing the fight.

The viscount began to talk about the gardens at the back of the house, saying work was to begin on them the next day and the summerhouse would perhaps be torn down.

When the servants had retired, Jean said, "Thank you so much for this necklace. I cannot help, however, thinking that perhaps it might be too grand a gift for a governess."

He considered the matter. "I suppose it is. Still, you need not wear it in company if you think it will occasion comment."

For some reason this practical solution hurt Jean, and she said waspishly, "I fear my reputation has been ruined."

He smiled at her over the rim of his wineglass. "Who's the lucky fellow?"

"I am not funning, my lord. On leaving your bedroom this morning, or, rather, early afternoon, I was seen by Lady Conham and Miss Eliza."

"Were you now. That must have poured cold water on the marital ambitions of that family."

Jean said in a thin voice, "But as far as they were concerned, you had been taking your pleasure with a servant, and *that* will not put any ambitious mama off. But the question of my reputation is another matter."

"Of course it is," he said. "I'll write to the Conham woman. The story of the smugglers is all over the county by now, so it will be easy to explain what you were doing in my room." His eyes teased her. "Was my bed comfortable?"

"My lord, we must talk of serious matters. I am flattered that you have asked me to dine with you, but should not the Misses Courtney be also present?"

"No, Miss Morrison. I shall dine in solitary state from now on, but this evening I felt like indulging myself. Besides, we must talk of the girls' future. Even before the smuggling episode I had been considering the possibility that I might have to send them away if they proved to be actually villainous—which they have. I was asking my guests about various places, not letting them know, of course, that it was for the Courtney girls. So . . . it appears there is in Bath a highly successful seminary for young ladies who have strayed from either the path of the law or the path of morality. It is a rigorous regime, more like a genteel prison, but they appear to get results."

Jean leaned forward and clasped her hands together. "My lord, as I said, I am sure they are truly penitent. Think for a moment how easy it was for such a man as Perdu to lead them astray. I gather their father loved them and indulged them, but he did not actually have anything much to do with them. He allowed them to rout a series of poor governesses and then let them run wild. So, bored, and with empty minds, and no refinements of speech or manners, they were easy prey for such as Perdu. He could be very charming. He supplied them with interest and adventure, and I think both were a little in love with him."

"What is your experience of love, Miss Morrison?"

"My lord, I am being deadly serious."

"And a bit of a bore, too. The fact that I didn't shoot that pair as well as Perdu amazes me. Oh, very well, what are your plans for Goneril and Regan?"

"They are still children and *not* like King Lear's

daughters," Jean said severely. "My lord, give me a little more time with them and I am sure the improvement will amaze you."

"Any improvement would amaze me. It actually does look quite well by candlelight."

"My lord?"

"Your lace. But there is a lace box somewhere. Ask Mrs. Moody. She'll give you the lace book and the key to the box. Keep it locked, or the girls will be selling priceless lace behind your back in order to buy chocolates."

"My lord, such a box should be kept for your bride along with the jewels."

"Do you think so? Oh, well, take some of it and then score off what you have taken in the lace book."

Well, what was he supposed to say? thought Jean bleakly. *I shall never marry. I want to marry* you.

But some imp prompted her to ask, "Do you intend to marry, my lord?"

"I suppose I ought to. Lots of fine girls at that ball of mine. But I couldn't see one of them *here*. Not walking about or sitting at table in the evenings with me. I picture the lady I want as my wife tall, I think, and beautiful, smiling graciously, but she is always silent in my dreams, for the minute I imagine her speaking to me, I conjure up the sound of bad French or lisping baby-talk or any of the other horrors they go in for. Who is the man of your dreams, Miss Morrison?"

What if she said someone like you? "Oh, tall, strong, noble, intelligent, worthy, serious, kind," Jean said, ticking off the virtues on her fingers.

"I'm tired," he said crossly, "and you are not enlivening the evening by singing the virtues of some puritan bore. Talk about something else."

"What do you wish me to talk about?"

"Miss Morrison, were you never taught to flirt?"

"Of course, my lord, it is part of every young lady's education. But governesses do not flirt with employers, not unless they wish to face a life of ruin."

"Really . . ." he said peevishly, "if you go on in this vein, I will need to cut off your supply of novels."

Jean rose to her feet. "I will leave you to your wine, my lord."

"Have I given you permission to leave?"

"No, my lord."

"Then sit down."

Jean sat down, staring at him wide-eyed. What if he made some sort of advance? Could she resist him?

"Rhododendrons, I think," he said.

"I beg your pardon?" Jean looked at him stupidly.

"For the gardens at the back," he said patiently. "Here, I'll explain. It's been a sort of terracing. It would be pleasant to have a winding walk bordered by rhododendrons going down to the beach. Perhaps the gardener can get some without going all the way to India. I'm sure he could get some out of Pemberton's gardener. And fuchsia. Statuary, too. I don't know much about trees and flowers."

"You need a proper landscape gardener," Jean said. "He would know exactly which trees and plants to use and how to create vistas."

"Good idea. I'll get Stewart, if he'll come. His reputation is now almost as high as that of Capability Brown. But the men can begin clearing the

135

mess tomorrow." He talked on about his plans while Jean slowly relaxed. At last he said, "You may retire, Miss Morrison."

"And will you give me some time to improve the girls?"

"Yes, if you must. But do not let them out of your sight, or, rather, when you are not with them, make sure someone is guarding them."

He walked around and drew Jean's chair back as she stood up. She smelled of rosewater and soap. He kissed her hand and felt it tremble in his own. He straightened up and looked down into her green eyes, his own suddenly watchful, as if searching for something. Then his gaze fell to her lips.

Jean stared up at him, trapped helplessly in that blue gaze. To her horror, large tears welled up in her eyes.

He drew back immediately. "I had forgotten your recent ordeal," he said gently, "and I am a beast to tease you so. Old habits die hard, Miss Morrison. Forgive me."

Jean curtsied and left. She trailed up the stairs, thinking sadly that he had certainly explained his behavior. She was the only woman present, and he had automatically flirted with her.

Betty was sitting guard outside the girls' door. "Lock them in and leave them for the night," Jean said wearily.

Inside, Amanda heard the click of the key in the lock and nudged Clarissa. "Remember," she whispered. "Good as gold and I'll have her forgetting to lock that door in no time at all!"

The next few weeks were for Jean the happiest she had ever experienced. The twins worked hard.

Their rough voices were being transformed, they began to read well and to write proper English. She rode or walked with them in the afternoons, and although they did not talk to her very much, Amanda would sometimes take her hand and even on one occasion gave her an impulsive hug. The viscount was impressed at the improvement and said so. It was an Indian summer of the kind so rarely seen in England, long, mellow days and cold, starry nights.

Although Jean did not dine with the viscount again, he often joined her in the drawing room after dinner and sat and listened while she read to the girls or played the piano.

And then one evening he announced he was going to London. Jean's heart sank. London and Nancy. London and his friends. London and parties and routs and dances. What if he came back with a bride?

With a heavy feeling in her breast she stood outside a few mornings later and watched him drive off, experiencing a numbing sensation of loss.

That evening she visited the girls as usual, but was startled when she was leaving to hear Amanda cry plaintively, "You don't trust us. We try so hard, but you don't love us. Nobody has ever loved us."

"But you are doing so well and I am proud of you both!" Jean cried.

"Then why do you lock us in like prisoners?"

Jean hesitated. But she thought Amanda was in the right. She must become their friend, and she could not do that while they still regarded her as their jailer. "Very well," she said. "I trust you. You will not be locked in again."

"And that settles that," Amanda crowed when Jean had left. "Now for Basil Devenham."

A week later Basil rode along the coast toward Trelawney Castle, wondering why on earth the Misses Courtney had summoned him. He was to meet them on the beach below the castle. The grooms slept over the stables, and Amanda and Clarissa had decided it would be too risky to take out horses during the night. In order to deliver the letter to Basil they had previously walked all the way to the Pembertons' mansion and did not want to make such a walk again.

Basil, until he had received their letter, had given up hoping that Hunterdon might slip up in some way. He had tried to court one of the Pemberton girls, but without success, and now Lord Pemberton was hinting broadly that it was time he took his leave.

He hoped against hope that the Courtneys were going to complain to him about their treatment.

He saw them down on the beach, dismounted, tethered his horse, and made his way down the steep slope to where the two little figures stood side by side on the sand.

"I am come in answer to your letter," he said. There was half a moon shedding only a little light. Their faces were round disks pierced with the black holes of their eyes.

"We have a proposition to put to you," Amanda said.

"Which is?"

"How would you like half of the Courtney fortune? That is, half of the money and half of what the castle, estates, and farms are worth?"

"Well, of course I would," he said indulgently. "But I cannot gain any of the inheritance unless you complain of your treatment or are neglected in any way." He looked at them sharply. "Well . . . are you?"

"No."

"Why am I here, then?"

"Listen, fool," Amanda said. "It is of no use us complaining about our lot, for the lawyer would come from London and find that not to be the case. Hunterdon is the model guardian and the model landowner. So . . . you kidnap us and hold us for ransom."

"Monstrous!" Basil exclaimed. "Run home, little girls, and do not plague me again with your fantasies."

"Don't come hoity-toity with me," Amanda snapped. "Think on't. Without us Hunterdon cannot keep the estate. He loves the place. He would pay you half of everything in order to try to keep it. He don't like us, but he'll do his duty, particularly if you threaten to kill us."

"You must be mad. All Hunterdon would do would be to shoot me."

Amanda groaned. "Listen hard. Hunterdon wouldn't know it's you. He's in London just now and due back next week. We disappear, you find a place to look after us, a place no one can find. You write a letter demanding the ransom. We'll find a place for him to leave it."

"There's something wrong here." Basil tilted back his hat and scratched his head. "Do you mean I get this fortune and then you return? What do you get out of it?"

"Five percent's enough for us," Amanda said.

"But that governess will lose her post and be in disgrace, and Hunterdon will have a hard time of it trying to run those estates with little capital, so he might give them up finally. He's to be punished as well, d'ye see?"

"No, I don't. What's he done to you?"

"That's our business. But think on our plan—for what can go wrong? Who will suspect you?"

Basil shifted restlessly. He thought of all that money. That was the trouble. Money. He received only a small allowance from a family trust. He was sure that was why the Pemberton girl had snubbed him. With money he could get any woman he wanted. With money he could cut a dash in Town. Besides, what could go wrong? If nothing happened to his ransom demand—yes, he found he was beginning to think of it already as *his* ransom demand—he could simply tell the girls to go.

"When does this take place?"

"Within a few days. Find a secluded place first. This is Monday. Be at this spot at this time on Friday."

"Leave it all to me," Basil said, making up his mind.

By the time he returned to the Pembertons, he had more or less convinced himself that it had mostly been his planning. It was not as if he were being ordered and manipulated by a couple of little girls.

The following day Jean received a letter from the viscount. In it he said he would be arriving the following Monday with the lawyer who wished to make sure the Courtney girls were well cared for. He asked her if she would act as his secretary in the meantime, open all letters, and deal with his bills.

Jean decided not to tell the twins about the lawyer's forthcoming visit. They might become too nervous, she thought indulgently. She was proud of them as they were and did not want them overacting or showing off because of nervousness. Amanda had confided in Jean that the viscount's threat to send them both away still haunted them.

She set them some lessons, and leaving Betty in charge of the schoolroom she went down to the desk in the library and started to go through the viscount's correspondence. There were a few invitations to balls and parties to be held locally the following month. She put these separately in a neat pile. He would need to decide himself which to accept. There were no urgent or pressing bills, and so she decided these, too, could await his return, but she wrote down on a sheet of paper the sums demanded and to whom they were to be paid. There were two letters from friends, both male. She skimmed through the first few lines to make sure they were only social letters and not in need of any urgent reply. Then there was a heavily scented one with an ornate seal. She opened it. She read the first few lines and blushed scarlet before glancing at the signature at the bottom. Nancy! Nancy reminding the viscount of the pleasures of the bed and saying she was weary of her current lover.

Jean picked it up by one corner, carried it over to the fireplace, and dropped it in the grate. Then she lit it, watched it burn, and then pounded the blackened paper up with the poker.

Immediately afterward she felt miserable with guilt. He would have met Nancy in London, Nancy would tell him about the letter, and he would wonder where it was. Guilt seemed to grow as the day wore on, and even the exemplary behavior of Amanda and Clarissa did nothing to lessen it.

By Saturday morning Jean awoke in a calmer frame of mind. Challenged by him, she would lie. She had committed a sin in burning that letter, so what did one lie matter now? She would say that it must have been lost in the post.

She glanced at the clock. It was nine o'clock, later than the twins usually slept, but she had promised them not to disturb them until ten because it was Saturday.

She had just finished dressing, when Betty burst into the room, crying, "They're gone!"

Cold fear clutched Jean's heart and then she steadied herself. "How naughty of them," she said lightly. "I shall find them, never fear."

But after an hour of searching the grounds she began to panic. She told Dredwort to gather all the servants and tenants together in the hall. It took ages to get them all assembled. Jean, striving for calm, stood up on the stairs and addressed them. She told them the Misses Courtney were missing. She told them the terms of the will, that if there was any fault in the care of the girls, any sign of negligence, the house and estates would go to Lord Hunterdon's cousin, Basil Devenham, who, she believed, would ruin the estates as effectively as Mr. Courtney had ruined them. Therefore, they must all help in the search, but they were to make sure that no word of the girls' disappearance reached the ears of the Pembertons, where she believed Basil Devenham was still staying.

They all searched desperately through the day

and far into the night without success. The tenants saw the shadow of the poorhouse looming and were every bit as terrified as Jean. By Sunday evening there was still no trace of them.

Jean called them all together again. "We are ruined," she said flatly, "and may as well call the constable and magistrate and alert the militia. For the lawyer is coming with my lord tomorrow and there is no way we can keep this quiet."

There was a dismal silence, and then Farmer Tulley called, "I think there might be a way. My twin daughters, Bertha and Jane. They be fourteen but tall for their age, and they've got ladylike ways. Can play the piano and draw and suchlike. I'll bring 'em up to the castle and you present them to the lawyer as Miss Amanda and Miss Clarissa. Get his lordship aside and warn him not to look surprised and tell him what has happened and try to get rid of the lawyer sharpish."

There was a murmur of approval. No one was frightened for the welfare of the girls, who were generally detested, and all believed they were hiding somewhere just in order to create mischief.

"Of all the *stupid* ideas," Amanda said for what seemed like the hundredth time, and Basil glared at her balefully.

He himself thought he had been very clever. He had paid a gypsy a handsome sum for the use of his caravan for a few weeks. It was hidden in the glades of Chomley Wood, which lay some twenty miles to the east of the castle. He had always romantically fancied himself in gypsy clothes. He had thought the girls would enjoy the setting. But Amanda and Clarissa had cried out at the lack of servants, at the cramped accommodation, at the boredom of being stuck in the center of the woods. They expected him therefore to be their servant, cooking all the meals and doing all the chores. They treated him with open contempt, and Basil could only pray that the reply to the ransom demand which Hunterdon would receive on Monday morning in his post bag would be quick.

The girls seemed to demand a great deal of food, and he was tired of the long journey to St. Giles to fetch even more provisions. Dressing as a gypsy he found was not romantic at all, and some people spat on him in the street. With all the business of cooking over an open fire, he was rapidly becoming as smelly and dirty as the gypsy he was supposed to be, and his white hands were callused with chopping wood.

Also, Amanda and Clarissa, who had been used to their well-structured days under Jean Morrison's rule, found time lying heavy on their hands and tried to enliven it by playing tricks on him, like putting grass snakes in his bunk bed, or climbing trees and dropping things on his head when he walked underneath. The last object had been a sharp stone that had gashed his forehead.

The viscount arrived in the middle of the morning on Monday. He was glad the lawyer could see how popular he was as a landlord when he drove through the estates, for people kept running toward the carriage, waving frantically. The viscount could not know that everyone was trying to warn him about the situation. So he waved back merrily as the carriage bowled rapidly in the direction of the castle.

His butler met him at the door and said urgently, "A word in private, my lord."

"Later, Dredwort. Show Mr. Broome to his quarters."

"As a matter of fact," Mr. Broome said, "I would like to see the Misses Courtney before anything else."

"Very well. Where are they, Dredwort?"

"In the drawing room, my lord, but . . ."

"Come along, Mr. Broome," the viscount said. "Stop hovering, Dredwort, and see that Mr. Broome's bags are carried upstairs."

A footman stood in front of the double doors of the drawing room. "My lord," he said in anguished tones, "if I might have a word?"

"Stand aside, James. When I have attended to Mr. Broome's affairs, you may have all the time you want."

The footman slowly opened the doors and moved aside.

The viscount stood on the threshold. Jean Morrison was there with two young ladies whom he recognized as the Tulley girls. He opened his mouth to speak, but Jean forestalled him firmly by saying, "This must be Mr. Broome. Amanda! Clarissa! Make your curtsies."

The dandy was often compared to the American Indian for his capacity to maintain a perfectly blank face during times of stress and pain. So with every appearance of complacent calm, the viscount watched the Tulley girls make their curtsies.

"Good day, ladies," Mr. Broome said. "Now, Miss Amanda . . . ?"

Bertha Tulley stepped forward.

"How is your schooling progressing?"

"Very well, zurr," Bertha said. "We do have a goodly knowledge of mathematics as well as English and French."

"Very good, very good. A bit of a country accent there, hey, Miss Morrison?" Mr. Broome had already been told the name of this governess of distinction.

"Yes, that will soon be eradicated," Jean said. "The poor girls were barely literate when I arrived, and so I decided to leave the problem of speech until later."

"Quite right, quite right," Mr. Broome agreed, growing more indulgent by the minute. He thought Jean Morrison looked all a governess should be with her hair scraped up into a cap and wearing a severe gown, and the Tulley girls were very pretty with rosy cheeks and thick blond hair, not at all what he had expected.

"And Miss Clarissa?" Jane stepped forward. "Do you play the pianoforte yet?"

"Oh, yes, Mr. Broome. Miss Morrison do be ever such a good teacher."

She sat down at the piano and played a simple piece of music very competently.

"Well, well," Mr. Broome said, "I am most pleased, most pleased. Now, if I may retire to my room for a nap, my lord? I am an old man, and long journeys tire me, and as you know, I must travel on to Poole on the morrow to see my niece."

Jean put her head in her hands when the lawyer had left with the viscount. Then she said, "You did splendidly, both of you. You may do as you please to amuse yourselves, but stay within call in case you are needed again."

146

When the Tulley girls had left, Jean sat and waited. She did not have long to wait.

The door crashed open and the viscount strode in, followed by a babbling Dredwort and a crying Mrs. Moody. "You tell me," he said, towering over Jean.

In a dull, flat voice she told him of how they were missing, how she had found them gone on Saturday morning, of the frantic search, of how they had decided to have the Tulley girls impersonate Amanda and Clarissa for the lawyer's visit.

"And how did they manage to leave?" he asked, his voice loaded with sarcasm. "Did brigands come in the night and drag them away? I found the spare key to their room which they had hidden and confiscated it. How?"

Jean hung her head. "I had not been locking them in."

"Why?"

"Amanda said it showed a lack of trust." Jean raised heavy eyes. "I thought they were fond of me."

"You silly widgeon. You nincompoop. Oh, let me think. I shall be in the library if that curst lawyer wants me."

But in the library he found the letter. It was lying on top of the morning's post, and something about it and the fact it had only a plain seal made him open it. It demanded half the Courtney inheritance for the safe return of the Misses Courtney. He swore under his breath.

He marched back up to the drawing room, but it was empty. He went to Jean's room and there she was, facedown on the bed, sobbing.

"Oh, get up!" he shouted. "I need help to think,

and I can't think with you caterwauling about the place."

Jean sat up abruptly, rage drying the tears on her cheeks, thinking of all the worry on his behalf, all the plotting and planning and all he could do was shout at her.

"Now," he said, sitting down on the bed and throwing a casual arm about her shoulders as he dragged her closer, "read that."

Jean read the short letter. " 'If you do not bring a sum of money equivalent to half the Courtney fortune and place it in Dead Man's Oak at the western corner of Chomley Wood by Saturday, I will kill the Misses Courtney.' "

"Kidnapped!" Jean looked at him wide-eyed, forgetting both rage and grief in her amazement. He gave her a little shake. "Think. Let us think. Observe the writing style. Educated and literate. 'The Misses Courtney' mark you. Not 'the young ladies.' Could those hellcats have thought up this scheme?"

"I cannot believe it," Jean said. "They have been so good, so very good. Besides, what can two young girls do with the money?"

"Yes, there is that. They have not been abducted by force. No signs of a struggle?"

"Perhaps there are more smugglers," Jean said with a shiver. "Perhaps one of them crept up to their room during the night and held a pistol to their heads to make them go quietly."

"Whoever it was would have had to be a bold man indeed. They left by the front door. In fact, Dredwort said he found the hall door unlocked and unbolted and standing wide open. I'm sure they are behind this. If only I could be really sure. Do you know what I would do?"

Jean shook her head dumbly.

"I'd let them rot," he said savagely.

"Oh, but they may be in deadly peril. They were so affectionate. Amanda even hugged me."

"I'll find them. I am sure I shall when I get rid of this curst lawyer. But why the Tulley girls? I cannot be blamed if they are being held for ransom, or appearing to be held for ransom, and I have the letter to prove it."

"I did think they might just have run away," Jean said. "The lawyer was coming. I had to do something."

He stared down at the letter again. "Chomley Wood," he said slowly. "I'll bet that's where they're hiding out, and that's where I'll be tonight as soon as Broome goes to sleep."

"Take me with you," Jean begged. "If I have been duped by them, I would feel better if I helped to find them."

"No, you have done enough," he said nastily. He gave her a little shake and then dropped a casual kiss on her nose. "Your eyes are all red with crying," he said. "You look a fright."

And so Jean Morrison cried a great deal more after he had left the room.

The viscount rode out that night at the head of a small army of cottagers, farmers, and servants. They had been told to dismount—those that were on horseback—and fan out in the woods on foot. It was a bright moonlit night, and they had all been told not to show any torches.

He thought about the evening's dinner. If he got out of this mess, then he would reward Farmer Tulley and his girls. They had behaved superbly. And

Jean Morrison? He had been too harsh with her. She had behaved like a Trojan and with great loyalty. No longer would she need to worry about her future. He would give her a dowry and a generous allowance. With her unusual beauty she would soon find a husband.

When they all reached the outskirts of the woods, he dismounted, tethered his horse, and, whispering instructions to his "army" to be as quiet as possible, he moved softly into the darkness of the woods, searching and listening.

A twig cracked behind him, and he swung around, but there was nothing there, just darkness lit by the odd shaft of moonlight. He reached a clearing and turned around. There was a sort of scuffling sound behind him and then silence. He strode across the clearing quickly and then darted behind the thick trunk of an oak and looked in all directions. A slight figure ran lightly across the clearing and then stopped quite near him. Whoever it was, he could hear him breathing. He moved gently and softly toward the sound until he saw a dark figure just at the edge of the clearing. He removed his pistol from his pocket and leveled it. "Walk into the clearing," he ordered. "I am holding a gun on you. Put your hands above your head."

The figure—a boy?—did as it was bid.

"Now let's see who you are," he said.

"It is I, my lord," a shaky voice answered.

He strode forward.

"Miss Morrison?"

"Yes," she whispered.

She was wearing breeches, a shirt, and a leather waistcoat, and had her thick hair pushed up under a cap. Jean had found the clothes in one of the trunks in the attic.

"What on earth do you think you are doing?"

"I feel it is all my fault," she said wretchedly. "I wanted to help."

"Go home. You are not helping at all. This is no place for a woman."

"Let me come with you," she begged. "I have sharp senses." He opened his mouth to protest, but she held up her hand and sniffed the air. "There! Do you smell it?"

"I smell trees and grass."

"Smoke. Old smoke. Like the smell of a fire after it has been put out. Follow me."

She slid quietly into the shelter of the trees, and he followed. She stopped every now and then and sniffed the air, moving all the time slowly forward. And then he could smell it, too, the faint acrid tang of smoke in the air.

He hooted like an owl, the signal to the other searchers that he was on the track of something. Jean moved noiselessly forward. Sometimes he thought she was mistaken, that she had lost the way, but she walked silently and steadily, the smell of smoke and ashes becoming stronger. He could sense the dark shapes of the other searchers closing about them and hooted softly this time to let them know where he was. He was answered by a volley of hoots, and he cursed inwardly. If there were people close by, they would think it odd that the woods were suddenly full of owls.

Jean was beginning to wonder whether she might be mistaken when the trees fell back and there was a glade in front of her, and in the glade, a gypsy caravan.

* * *

Basil stirred uneasily and then woke. There were a lot of noisy owls hooting. He cursed the countryside and all in it. The caravan was close and smelly, and the worst of the smell was coming from the Misses Courtney. They were still wearing the clothes in which they had arrived, the clothes they had subsequently played in, climbed trees in, and slept in.

He could never last until the end of the week, he thought miserably, not in such company. They were evil. He was tired of their white faces, their beady little eyes, and their endless greed. He had never known that two young ladies could eat so much. His hand was sore where he had burnt it on the cooking pot. He had stumbled when Amanda had playfully tried to push him into the fire and he had saved himself from falling by grabbing the edge of the large pot. Although he affected to have high morals and a strong religious belief, he had hitherto not believed in any supernatural presence. But now he prayed feverishly to the God he hoped existed, after all, to get him out of this mess.

He decided to go outside and savor the presence of a midnight world that was not polluted with either the smell or the horrible pranks of the Courtney girls.

He opened the door, stood on the step of the caravan, and stretched and yawned.

Then there came the scraping sound of a tinderbox. In the glade one torch sprang into life, then another. He trembled. All around the glade were men, men who were closing in.

The tallest walked forward in the moonlight. He

recognized his cousin, Hunterdon, and let out a bleat of fear.

"Who are you, Gypsy, and what are you doing here?" the viscount demanded.

Gypsy? Of course Hunterdon couldn't recognize him. He broke into gibberish which he fondly hoped they would believe to be Romany. "Dish bonker iddle tum?"

The viscount seized a pine torch from one of the men, walked forward, and held it up.

"Basil," he said in tones of loathing.

"Iggle dimp zuz boo," Basil said desperately.

"Drag him down and tie him up," the viscount ordered. He said to Jean, "Come with me."

Jean followed him up the steps of the caravan as the howling Basil was dragged down onto the grass and bound.

The viscount opened the door. The twins were sleeping heavily. In the light of the torch Jean saw them clearly. They were lying side by side on a narrow bunk, wrapped in each other's arms.

"And there, if I am not mistaken, are the ones who thought up this scheme," the viscount said.

"Perhaps he coerced them," Jean protested. "They look so innocent. . . ."

And then Amanda opened her eyes. Jean had removed her cap, and her red hair tumbled about her shoulders. Amanda's sleepy eyes widened in surprise as they focused on Jean, and then became filled with such a look of pure hate that Jean took a step back.

"Go outside," the viscount said to Jean. "Go quickly. I do not want you or that soft heart of yours anywhere near them."

Jean stumbled outside and sat down on the grass wearily.

She heard the viscount call something, and several of the men went into the caravan.

Her head felt heavy, and she realized she was deathly tired. She lay down on the grass. Let the viscount cope with it all. It was too much for her. She closed her eyes and fell fast asleep.

The viscount gave orders that the girls were to be bound and confined in the caravan under guard until the lawyer had left. Basil was to be put with them. As soon as he was shot of the lawyer, then caravan and prisoners were to be pulled to the castle.

The men were warned that the girls would probably try every trick in the book to escape.

The viscount shook Jean awake. "On your feet, Miss Morrison. I will escort you home."

Jean rose and stumbled. He put a strong arm around her waist. Holding her close, he led her through the woods, one of the cottagers striding ahead with a blazing torch to light the way.

"I hope he knows where he is going," Jean said.

"His name is Connan. He knows these woods."

"Where is your horse?" he asked.

"I walked," Jean said. "I saw you moving off, so I slipped out of the castle and joined those on foot."

"No wonder you are exhausted. My hunter can bear both of us." He threw her up into the saddle and then mounted behind her. "Riding astride and in breeches, Miss Morrison," he mocked. "Fie for shame."

Jean sat silently, conscious of his arm around her waist, thinking that she must give up expecting life to be like books. In a book it would not have been tame Basil but some real villain. The viscount would have been overcome by her courage and fortitude. Riding through this beautiful moonlit night, he would have whispered endearments in her ear, not mocked her in that infuriatingly frivolous way of his. Nor would he suddenly spur his horse so that they were speeding through the silent countryside instead of ambling romantically under the moon.

Outside the castle he dismounted and held up his arms, and she slid down wearily into them. "First," he said, smiling down at her, his eyes glittering in the moonlight, "and before I speak to you further, I have to deal with more important matters."

"Such as?"

"I must rub down my horse. Poor old Harry is sweating like a pig. Wait for me in the drawing room."

She went wearily up to her room, thinking inconsequently that he did not think of her as a lady. No gentleman ever talked about sweat in front of a lady.

Betty was waiting for her, and as soon as she had silently helped Jean to wash and change into a gown, Mrs. Moody scratched at the door, begging to be told the news. Jean told the housekeeper to go to the drawing room, and by the time she had joined her there, Dredwort and the other members of the staff who had not joined in the hunt were waiting anxiously.

Jean told them all what had happened, and then, turning to Betty, said, "Mr. Broome will expect to see the girls in the morning. Have them washed and dressed and downstairs by eight, and make sure you wake me first!"

The viscount arrived and the servants filed out, leaving Jean alone with him.

"As soon as the lawyer has gone," he said abruptly, "I am dealing with Basil and then getting that precious pair on the road to Bath to that special seminary." He held up his hand, seeing she was about to speak. "No, Miss Morrison, you are not going with us. They will trick you again or do their best to. Now, as to your future."

Jean clasped her hands in front of her and gazed at him, her eyes wide. "I am much indebted to you. You have endured more perils than any respectable governess should expect to suffer. I shall make you a generous allowance and give you a good dowry. I have an aunt in London, Lady Baxter, who is kind and gentle. I shall write to her on my return and ask her if she will chaperone you during a London Season. It should be easy for you to find a husband."

Color rose in Jean's cheeks. "Thank you," she said faintly. She should be so grateful to him, but inside, a little childlike voice was wailing that she did not want to leave him.

"So you have one more ordeal. We must all act out our parts at breakfast until Mr. Broome leaves. Then I would advise you to sleep as much as you can. Handle my letters and bills. Connan—the man who led us back—his wife is poorly. Ride over and see if she needs the attention of the physician. Mr. Peterman, the agent, will take any orders from you. The men are to go ahead with the work on clearing the gardens at the back. Stewart will be arriving soon with plans for the landscaping but probably not until after my return. I know now Amanda and Clarissa thought up the ransom scheme and lured

Basil into it. He is too stupid to have thought up such a thing himself. In return for his perfidy, he will sign a statement renouncing any possible claim to the estates."

"What will become of the Courtney girls after their stay at the seminary is finished?" Jean asked.

"At the moment, I neither know nor care. Go to bed, Miss Morrison."

But he did not rise or kiss her hand. He stayed slumped in his chair as she sadly left the room.

Chapter Eight

THE VISCOUNT ARRIVED at the seminary on the outskirts of Bath three days later. Amanda and Clarissa had enlivened the journey by begging and pleading, cajoling and crying, and had finally settled for sulky abuse. They said loudly that he was getting rid of them only so that he could take his pleasure with his whore, Jean Morrison.

He left them in his carriage under guard while he went into the seminary to talk to the principal. He was taken aback. She was a roly-poly, jolly woman wearing a purple silk dress and a huge starched cap. Her voice was somewhat coarse. He knew her to be a Mrs. Davey, but that was all he knew about her.

Her study was ornamented with pretty, spindly furniture and a quantity of bric-a-brac. A long window looked out onto a pleasant garden. He noticed that the window was not barred, and wondered how this woman could keep such a villainous pair as Amanda and Clarissa Courtney incarcerated, or, in fact, do anything with them.

After welcoming him, Mrs. Davey said, "You are lucky we have room for two more, my lord. I knew from your letter that you were contemplating placing your wards with us, but you did not warn us of when you were coming or if you were coming."

"I must warn you that my wards are criminals," the viscount said. He settled back and told Mrs. Davey of their smuggling and of their subsequent attempt to appear to have been abducted.

She nodded placidly when he had finished. "Are they virgins?"

He looked at her in surprise. "They are fifteen years."

"And there are younger prostitutes than that on the streets of London, as you very well know, my lord."

"I do not know if they are virgins or not," he said. He eyed her doubtfully. "This seems a pleasant place, Mrs. Davey, not what I expected. Perhaps you do not realize that Amanda and Clarissa should really be in prison."

A neat servant brought in a tray of tea and cakes, curtsied, and left.

Mrs. Davey poured tea. Then she took out a squat gin bottle and calmly topped up her teacup with a shot before holding the bottle out enquiringly to the viscount, who refused.

"You know my fees?" Mrs. Davey asked.

"Yes."

"So . . . very expensive, ain't they?"

"I noticed that."

"Well, the reason they are expensive is that I produce successes here. If I did not, no one would send their girls to me. All of them should be in prison, but they come from genteel families who hope to save them. I profit. Bring 'em in and let me have a look at them."

The viscount went out and returned with Amanda and Clarissa. Mrs. Davey added more gin to her cup and stared at them. She shrugged her fat shoulders. "Nothing out of the common way. Leave them with me, my lord. You will receive quarterly reports. No, I beg of you, do not look so worried. I can cope with anything."

When the viscount had left, Mrs. Davey, still staring at the two girls, rang the bell on the table beside her and told the maid who answered its summons to fetch Mrs. Grimshaw.

Mrs. Grimshaw turned out to be a tough, wiry, middle-aged woman with a sharp, knowing face. She looked more like a male horse trader than a female schoolmistress.

"Got two new 'uns," Mrs. Davey said. She looked at Clarissa. "Name?"

"Clarissa," she mumbled.

"So the one with the eyebrows must be Amanda. Right, Mrs. Grimshaw, Clarissa looks the softer one. She's to start work in the dairy and keep her at it for a year. The other one, Amanda, is to start work in the carpentry shop right away."

"This is slave labor," Amanda cried. "We are not peasants."

"No, lovey. Just be thankful you ain't on the treadmill in prison, where you belong. You're the ringleader. I've met your sort before ... many times. You will not be able to communicate with your sister at all, at any time. Now, get to work."

"Shan't!" Amanda shouted.

Mrs. Grimshaw twisted Amanda's arm up her back and marched her from the room. Clarissa cast Mrs. Davey a terrified look and hurried after her sister.

Mrs. Davey poured more gin into what was left

of the mixture in her cup and sank back with a satisfied sigh. Nothing like decent, honest work to bring her young ladies up to the mark and to make a good profit. Her cheeses were already selling well, there was a steady demand for the chairs and tables produced by the carpentry shop, the weaving shed was doing fine business, and the school farm was prosperous. Only the most hardened of the girls were put to farm labor, and Mrs. Davey did not consider Amanda and Clarissa anything particularly bad, just tiresome and naughty.

A few days later Jean Morrison found she had the delicate task of entertaining Lord and Lady Pemberton and their daughters, Letitia and Ann, delicate because although she was running the household, her position was still that of governess.

Letitia had persuaded her parents to make the call. She said it was ridiculous that such an eligible bachelor should be left unchallenged.

But when they arrived, Dredwort told them that Lord Hunterdon was not at home. Lady Pemberton said crossly that they would like some refreshment before their return journey, and Dredwort ushered them into the Green Saloon and then went to inform Jean of their arrival.

As soon as she entered and began to supervise the serving of tea and cakes, Jean realized her mistake. She should not have joined them. Lady Pemberton was glaring at Jean's pretty gown and uncapped hair and demanding to know where the Misses Courtney were. Jean had no intention of telling them about the seminary. She merely said quietly that they were visiting relatives of the viscount.

"Shouldn't you be in the schoolroom?" Letitia demanded waspishly.

"Not when I have no one to teach. What is it, Dredwort?"

"The agent, Mr. Peterman, has called, miss, and wishes to consult you about the work in the gardens, and Mr. Connan has ridden over to thank you for sending the physician to his wife. She is improving rapidly."

"Thank you, Dredwort. Good day, my lord, my lady, ladies. If there is anything further you require, please ring the bell."

The Pembertons looked at each other in consternation when she had left. "She is behaving like the mistress of this house," Lady Pemberton cried. "Has Hunterdon lost his wits?"

As if on cue, the gentleman in question entered the room. The viscount had returned.

"You must excuse my clothes," he said after the initial courtesies were over. "I am just returned from Bath."

"And I must inform you of something," Lady Pemberton said. "That Scotch governess is going on here as if she is mistress of this house and estates, and the servants appear to treat her as such."

"I left her in charge."

"How odd!" Lady Pemberton bridled.

Lord Pemberton shot her a warning look as if to say that she would not further her daughters' chances with the viscount if she questioned his domestic arrangements, however odd they might seem. He began to talk of mutual acquaintances and of the prospects of good hunting weather to come.

The viscount half listened, wishing they would

162

all go away. There was so much to do. Besides, he wanted to tell Miss Morrison about the seminary. He wanted to look at Miss Morrison again. He had thought of her a great deal on the road back. His comfortable feeling that he had secured her future for her was waning fast as he approached Trelawney. He tried to imagine Jean at her social debut, at Almack's, say, dancing the waltz and trying discreetly to attract the attentions of some suitable man. Then he had a sudden vision of going up to that suitable man and punching him on the nose for daring to put his arm around Jean Morrison's slender waist.

And it *was* a slender waist, he thought dreamily. And her eyes were fascinating, green and clever, like a cat's.

He suddenly realized all the Pembertons were staring at him. "My husband was asking you for the second time whether you plan to be in London for the next Season?" Lady Pemberton said.

He looked at her rather stupidly. Next Season. He could dance with Miss Morrison himself. That would be fun. But dammit, he had her here, under his nose. Could she be his? He felt a great feeling of relief wash over him and half closed his eyes. The horrible girls were gone. Trelawney was all peace and serenity. And he could have Jean Morrison to himself.

"Go away," he said loudly.

Lady Pemberton rose with a rustle of taffeta. "You will never hear from us again, my lord," she said. "I think you are quite mad."

"Yes, yes," he snapped. He beat them to the door, opened it, and darted up the stairs.

She wasn't in her room. She wasn't in the drawing room. Where!

He ran downstairs again as the Pembertons were making their stately exit. "Where is she?" he shouted to Dredwort.

"At the back of the house with Mr. Peterman, my lord."

The viscount shot out of the door. The Pembertons stared after him. Lady Pemberton saw Dredwort standing with a smile on his face. She curled an imperative finger. "Come here, my man, I have a few questions I wish to ask you about your master."

But Dredwort listened at doors and Dredwort had heard what Lady Pemberton had said in the Green Saloon about his master being mad. He carefully placed one thumb on his nose and wriggled the rest of his fingers in her direction. Then, patting his new glass wig with a complacent hand, he stalked down the stairs to tell Mrs. Moody that the champagne should be put on ice in preparation for the announcement of my lord's forthcoming marriage.

He found her standing with Mr. Peterman. Men were cutting down and hauling away briars and bushes. "I think the summerhouse should be left standing," he heard Jean say. "Perhaps Mr. Stewart, the landscape gardener, might want it to remain. My lord! You are returned."

"Walk with me a little, Miss Morrison," he said. "Mr. Peterman, I shall see you presently."

He held out his arm, and Jean hesitatingly laid her fingertips on it as he led her down the now-cleared walk toward the beach.

Her light dress fluttered against her body. The

wind from the sea was cold. She shivered slightly. "I unfortunately acted as hostess to the Pembertons," she said, glancing up at him and thinking miserably that he looked handsomer than ever. He had endured a tiring journey and yet he was impeccably dressed in blue coat, doeskin breeches, and top boots.

"Why unfortunately?"

"They considered it an impertinence."

"Boring family. Any family who can suffer Basil for any length of time must be boring." They reached the beach. "Are you cold?" he asked.

"A little. When Dredwort told me that Mr. Peterman wanted to see me, I was so glad to escape that I ran straight out of the house."

He stopped and took off his coat and put it around her shoulders. "Better?"

"Thank you, my lord, but I can quite easily return and find a shawl."

"Never mind. Let me tell you about the seminary." Jean listened as he described Mrs. Davey.

"Are you sure she can cope?" Jean asked anxiously.

"Strangely enough, I feel sure she can." The air was full of the sound of the restless sea. Waves crashed on the beach and the wind whipped through Jean's red hair, scattering bone pins onto the sand.

"I cannot help feeling sorry for them." Jean stared out to sea. "Life would have been better for them if their mother had not died. Their father, with his greed and his cruelty, was no example. A little love in their upbringing would have done wonders."

"You are too softhearted, my governess."

"Perhaps. Never having really known any love myself, I am perhaps oversympathetic."

"I would give you love."

Jean clutched his coat tighter around her shoulders. The wind whipped a strand of red hair across her lips, and he gently pulled it away. She looked up at him, her eyes filled with a mixture of misery and disgust.

He wanted her as his mistress.

She half turned away. "I do not want your love, my lord. I assume now your offer of allowance and dowry was a sham."

"No, by God, it wasn't," he said, suddenly furious with disappointment and longing. "The offer still stands. If you wish to be wife to some other man, you may do so gladly and with my blessing."

He walked away from her, back toward the castle, his shirtsleeves flapping against his arms.

She ran after him. His coat dropped from her shoulders to the beach, but she ran on.

"Stop!" she shouted, catching his arm and hanging on for grim death. "Do you want to *marry* me?"

"I've changed my mind anyway," he said pettishly. "Let go of my arm."

"You fool!" Jean screamed. "I thought you wanted me as your mistress."

He stopped abruptly. He looked at her intently, and then his eyes began to dance. "You have a smutty mind, Miss Morrison, not at all suitable in a governess. You shock me."

"Is this some game? Are you mocking me?"

"No, Miss Morrison, I can think of nothing I would like better. I shall get a special license and we will be married in, let me see, two weeks' time. It will need to be the little church in St. Giles, or the vicar can come to the house and marry us. Yes, perhaps that would be better. We shall have such splendid fun. How many children shall we have, do you think?"

She looked up at him pleadingly, her hands on his shoulders. "Do you really love me?"

He wrapped his arms around her and bent and kissed her full on the mouth. Her lips were cold and salty but gradually warmed under the insistent pressure of his own. He decided vaguely that kissing Jean Morrison was the most wonderful thing he had ever experienced, and so he continued to kiss her with increasing passion and force. Cold, stinging rain blew in from the sea, but neither of them felt it. He had all the single-mindedness of the aristocrat, and he had forgotten everything else about him. He drew her down onto the wet sand and held her tightly against him while his hands caressed her face and body with increasing urgency. He unfastened the little buttons at the front of her dress and kissed her breasts while her moans were whipped away by the salt wind.

And then a great, curling wave, racing ahead of its fellows on the fast incoming tide curled right over the passionate couple writhing in the sand. Jean gasped and choked and struggled upright, fumbling at the buttons on her wet dress, her face scarlet. Laughing, he stood up and pulled her to her feet. "I nearly forgot to wait until my wedding night," he said.

He put his arm around her waist and led her back to the castle, leaving his coat forgotten on the beach. "I know the servants will be pleased," he said. "We must make our announcement as soon as we are dry and changed."

But when they entered the great hall, wet and disheveled, they stopped at the sight of all the staff lined up in front of a trestle table that bore bottles of champagne, glasses, and ice from the icehouse.

"How did you know?" the viscount asked.

Dredwort grinned and slowly held up a small brass telescope. Jean blushed furiously and buried her hot face in the viscount's wet shirt.

"Then wait until we have changed, you reprobate," the viscount said with a grin.

The party went on for the rest of the day as tenants and farmers, estate workers and grooms, heard the news and came to drink the couple's health.

But Jean longed for them all to go away until she could be alone with him again.

The viscount, it turned out, had other plans.

"I have arranged for you to stay with Farmer Tulley until the wedding."

Jean looked at him in dismay. "But *why?*"

"Because if you stay here, I do not think I could stop myself from visiting your bedroom this night. I have told Tulley. I should write to my parents and invite my friends to this wedding, but I have decided to let it be just for us and the people of Trelawney. We can be married again in London later."

So Jean went reluctantly off with Mr. and Mrs. Tulley to sleep in a tiny room in the farm and wait for her wedding day.

She thought the days would drag past, but there was her dress to be made and all the preparations for the celebrations. Then Mrs. Tulley wanted to make use of this governess while she had her under her roof and had begged Jean to instruct her daughters in the social arts. Jean saw very little of the viscount, and when she did, she was strictly chaperoned by Mrs. Tulley. He was so light and cool and formal that Jean began to wonder whether he might be regretting his proposal.

And then she received a visit from Letitia and Ann Pemberton. The Pembertons had heard of the wedding plans, for all the shops in St. Giles were abuzz with the news as orders poured in from the castle. Letitia and Ann felt it was a direct snub. The viscount was the only eligible bachelor in the neighborhood, and he had shunned their beauty to marry a common Scotch governess. After some debate among themselves, they decided he was being forced to marry her to allay scandal. They wondered if Miss Morrison knew that and decided it would be better to tell her. They had called at the castle and learned where she was staying. Mrs. Tulley led them into the parlor and left them alone with Jean.

"We are come to felicitate you on your forthcoming marriage," Ann said haughtily.

"Thank you," Jean replied quietly.

"But we were also concerned for you. It must be sad to feel the groom is being constrained to marry you."

Jean forced a laugh. "Why should he feel that?"

"Well, all the gossip, you know. And Lady Conham and Eliza did see you leaving his ... er ... bedchamber." The viscount had remembered to write to Lady Conham explaining what Jean Morrison had been doing sleeping in his bed, and Lady Conham had dutifully spread the reason about, but neither Ann nor Letitia were going to let Jean know that.

Jean stood up, went to the door, and held it open.

"Be off with you," she said furiously. "Jealous, spiteful cats."

Letitia and Ann left well satisfied. For they knew by the mixture of fury and distress on Jean's face that some of the poison had sunk in.

Jean hardly knew what to do. She knew now that the viscount, for all his apparently frivolous ways, was a man with a strong sense of duty. The sensible and forthright thing would be to ask him outright. But then he might feel obliged to lie. He had kissed her with such passion, but he had not said he loved her or uttered one word of love in all that disgraceful writhing on the beach.

Her doubts tormented her right up to the wedding day, right up to the temporary altar that had been erected in the hall, and right up until he turned and looked down at her. His face was altered with love. She went through the responses, wondering whether she might faint from sheer happiness.

And then at last they were man and wife. The weather had turned dark and threatening, and scarlet and brown leaves whipped about the lawns in a crazy spiraling dance between the marquees that had been erected to shelter all the people of Trelawney estates. Everyone sang and danced. Dredwort made a speech, amazing for its pompous tone and salacious content. Mr. Tulley made a speech, forgot halfway through what he meant to say, and sat down abruptly. The viscount made a speech, thanking them all, and then, with Jean on his arm, left the festivities.

He led her up the great staircase. "Where are we going?" Jean asked, suddenly shy.

"To bed."

"In the middle of the afternoon! I am not tired."

"You will be, my sweeting. You will be."

In his bedchamber she stood before him, plucking at the stiff white folds of her gown with nervous fingers. "Why so downcast?" he teased. "Am I such an ogre?"

"I was thinking of the girls," she babbled. "I cannot help feeling they should have been here."

"Oh, no," he said. "At such a time and such a place. I refuse to think of those hellions. Come here. It's time you started thinking of me."

"Do . . . do you l-love me?"

"I am rampaging with love, I am *dying* with love. Kiss me! I will love you till the end of time, my Jean."

And she did kiss him, at first shyly, and then warmly, and then passionately until somehow she found herself in bed and under him without the least recollection of how her clothes had been removed.

Clarissa stood in the dairy beside the butter churn. She had been put in the charge of one of the older girls, a tall, sleepy blonde with a slow smile called Tabitha. "Finished?" Tabitha examined Clarissa's work. "Good," she said. "Very good."

Clarissa felt a glow of achievement. She had been told if she worked hard, then she might have gooseberry pie for dinner.

Over in the carpentry shop a young carpenter's apprentice, John Buxtable, was showing Amanda how to use a plane. He had an easygoing nature and laughed hard at all Amanda's tantrums. Amanda had tried to run away twice, but on both occasions she had been caught by staff, who were used to catching runaways. Initially she had been taught in the carpentry shop by a tall, morose girl who had complained bitterly to Mrs. Davey when Amanda had tried to stab her with a chisel.

Mrs. Davey had pondered over Amanda's character and had hired John Buxtable, a good-looking country boy. He had instructions to flirt a little with Amanda but not to go any further. And so as he showed her how to use the plane, he let his strong, brown, muscled arm brush against her own.

Amanda blushed and giggled.

Mrs. Davey, watching from the door with Mrs. Grimshaw, turned away. "I knew it would work," she said. "Nothing like a handsome, lusty man to bring a slut to heel!"